COLD MARKS THE SPOT

This is silly, Danny told himself. *There's nothing to be afraid of. Nothing.*

He took a step forward.

As soon as his foot touched the ground, it was as if he'd suddenly walked into a freezer. The air felt fifty degrees colder, and his body instantly became frozen on the spot. Jagged waves of coldness washed over him, like icicles being hammered into his body. His breath seemed to chill in his lungs. Then he couldn't breathe at all.

He was trapped where he stood, in a dead zone.

FOUL PLAY

TAG (YOU'RE DEAD)

BY JOHN PEEL

PUFFIN BOOKS

PUFFIN BOOKS
Published by the Penguin Group
Penguin Books USA Inc., 375 Hudson Street, New York, New York 10014, U.S.A.
Penguin Books Ltd, 27 Wrights Lane, London W8 5TZ, England
Penguin Books Australia Ltd, Ringwood, Victoria, Australia
Penguin Books Canada Ltd, 10 Alcorn Avenue, Toronto, Ontario, Canada M4V 3B2
Penguin Books (N.Z.) Ltd, 182–190 Wairau Road, Auckland 10, New Zealand

Penguin Books Ltd, Registered Offices: Harmondsworth, Middlesex, England

First published in the United States of America by Puffin Books,
a division of Penguin Books USA Inc., 1992

1 3 5 7 9 10 8 6 4 2

LIBRARY OF CONGRESS CATALOGING-IN-PUBLICATION DATA
Peel, John, 1954–
Tag (you're dead) / by John Peel.   p.   cm.—(Foul play; 2)
Summary: An ancient house becomes the perfect setting for a game
of tag, until a vengeful spirit with a touch of death joins the game.
ISBN 0-14-036053-0
[1. Supernatural—Fiction.] I. Title. II. Series:
Peel, John, 1954–   Foul play; 2.
PZ7.P348Tag 1992   [Fic]—dc20   92-19939

Printed in the United States of America
Set in Aster

TAG
(YOU'RE DEAD)

It was almost midnight. Zack wasn't sure how *he knew the time, but he did. There were a lot of things he didn't know, too. He didn't know why it looked so light even this late at night. He stared across his own overgrown yard to the neatly trimmed lawn of the house next door. He saw two tents in the backyard. In one were two girls, in the other two boys. For them, Zack knew, it was pitch-black. They were asleep now, but if they woke they would see the stars scattered across the rich blackness of the night.*

Zack hadn't seen a star in two hundred years. But one day . . . one day he'd see them again! He hadn't slept in two hundred years, either. He missed that. He missed a lot of things.

He moved closer to the other house. Then he felt the tightness in his chest that chained him to his own home. He paused. If he went farther the tight feeling would

1

become an iron fist to squeeze him and hurt him. It was now the only thing that could hurt him.

He looked into the next yard, almost able to feel the dreams of the sleeping kids there. He'd been watching them for days now. He'd always watched the two who lived there. Brandon was the boy. He was about eleven. And Nicole was . . . Zack thought for a moment. She was about nine, he realized. It was hard to believe she'd been around that long. Time had little meaning for Zack. He hadn't aged a day in two hundred years.

Things had been pretty quiet for a long time. Zack had become pretty bored watching Brandon and Nicole. And their friends from across the street. Adam and . . . Zack had to think for a minute. Tracy. That was it. He'd watched them playing games, listened to their laughter and arguments. He'd studied their silly way of talking. Sometimes he'd even mimicked it to himself, relishing the sounds of the new and different words. The language had been different back when Zack was forced to leave his world behind.

Now everything was different. The family next door had visitors—a husband and wife and their two children. It was summer, so they'd put up tents in the backyard. The kids seemed to be having a great time camping out.

Maybe it was because they were so close, without walls around them to protect them. Maybe it was that the two new children were special. Zack didn't know and he didn't really care. Whatever the reason, Zack was stirred by emotions he thought he'd forgotten.

2

Watching the kids play, he felt a tugging in his heart. He wished he could leave this house and its overgrown grounds. He wanted to shout and be heard. He wanted to throw a ball again. He wanted to join in the games he saw. He wanted to be alive again.

He stared across the fence that separated the two houses. Concentrating hard, Zack could almost feel the dreams flowing about him. Dreams that drifted through the minds of the four children who slept peacefully nearby.

Come to me, *Zack whispered into those stray, floating thoughts.* Come and play here. Come to me. . . . *He concentrated all of his energies into that single idea:* Come!

Tomorrow, perhaps, they would come.

Turning, Zack walked back to the old house. It was still standing, more from habit than from strength. The windows were boarded over. The doors were all nailed shut to stop anyone from getting in. None of that bothered Zack in the slightest. He passed through the solid wall and into the room beyond.

He'd wait for them.

They would come.

Chapter One

THE OLD HOUSE

Danny looked around the large, neatly cut lawn and sighed. He really missed Chicago. They had lived by the shore of the lake. There were lots of other kids his age around, and there was always something to do. Here in Breedon he felt trapped. Aside from his cousins, Brandon and Nicole, and his little sister, Kate, there were only two other kids near his age in the whole neighborhood.

He hated the idea that he'd have to get used to calling this boring little town home.

Now Kate and Nicole were with their friend Tracy McCall across the street. Brandon and Tracy's brother, Adam, were swapping baseball cards. Brandon didn't actually like baseball, but he loved the wheeling and dealing of trading valuable cards. Danny wandered over.

"I'm bored," he announced.

Brandon looked up at him.

"There's nothing to do," Danny complained. "I can't

4

even watch TV. They're all in there checking on houses for sale."

"You think you'll move far?" asked Brandon. He actually sounded like he hoped they wouldn't. Since his cousins had come to stay, Brandon had complained a lot, mainly about having to give up his room to Danny's parents. That's really why they were camping—the house was too small for two sets of parents *and* two sets of kids.

"I don't know," said Danny. "They won't tell me anything at all. But it won't be back to Chicago." Danny wished it could be, but he knew there was no chance. His father already had a job out here, and his mom was pretty hopeful that one of her interviews would work out. *They* were enjoying this, at least.

"Why don't we just stay here?" asked Kate, walking up to them with Nicole and Tracy. "It's fun."

"No way!" Brandon said emphatically. "There isn't room for all of us in our house."

Kate pointed to the two tents. "But we're not *in* the house. Don't you like camping out?"

Brandon shrugged. "Sure—for now. It's summer, and the weather's been nice. But what if it rains? Or snows? Besides, I want my own room back."

Danny thought it over. Brandon was right—camping was fun for a change, but you couldn't live like that forever.

"Dad and Mom could buy the old house," he said suddenly.

"Not!" Brandon shouted. "Even you wouldn't want to live there, buttbrain!"

5

Danny couldn't figure out why not. The old house next door had a gigantic yard—front and back. It looked like no one had lived there for years. The house was shabby and boarded up, and the lawns were choked with weeds and tall grass. But the house itself looked like it was still in good enough shape. And it was three stories tall, with a huge balcony on the top floor. Danny bet you could see for miles from up there.

"Why not?" he asked. "It looks like it would be kind of fun to live there."

"Not there," said Brandon firmly. "It's haunted."

Kate snickered. "Brandon Walker, you are such a liar!"

He turned red. "Am not," he snapped. "Ask anybody. It's haunted." He pointed to Adam, who had been silently sorting his baseball cards the whole time. "You tell them."

Adam shifted uncomfortably. "Yeah," he finally said. "It's really spooky there. People have seen things, you know?"

"Yeah, right," Danny muttered. He'd looked over at the house while Adam was talking. He couldn't explain it exactly, but as his eye had flickered over one of the boarded-up upstairs windows, he'd felt a sudden chill. He didn't believe in ghosts and haunted houses, and he knew it would sound weird, but it was almost like he felt a presence in the house.

He looked up again quickly, but nothing happened. "Get out, Brandon," he said as his confidence surged back. "You're so full of it."

"Uh-uh," Brandon insisted. "Tell you what—after we go to bed tonight, I'll tell you the story of the old house. You'll see." He grinned evilly. "Just the thing to give you pleasant dreams—not!"

"Yuk," said Kate, shuddering. "I don't like ghost stories."

"Scaredy cat," jeered Brandon.

"If you talk about ghosts," Tracy said, "it's like inviting them to haunt you. I don't think you should talk about Zack Powell."

"Right," Brandon grinned. "After all, he lives next door. If you can call it *living.* . . ."

Danny looked at the old house. There wasn't anything spooky about it. It was just old and abandoned. His chill of earlier hadn't come back.

Brandon caught him looking and gave him a big grin. "Wait till tonight," he promised. "I'll tell you the whole true, horrible, *bloody* story."

ZACHARY'S FATE

Later that night, when they were all ready for bed, Danny and Brandon moved their sleeping bags just inside the tent flap while Kate and Nicole did the same in their tent. Danny wriggled around to get comfortable, and then lay finally on his stomach, chin propped in his hands, elbows on the ground. Brandon had his sleeping bag wadded around his waist and sat there looking like the top half of a boy and the bottom half of a caterpillar.

Once Brandon was sure he had everyone's attention, he spoke. "This is the true and awful tale of the dark and dismal fate of Zackary Powell," he said in a hollow, echoing sort of voice.

"Get real," Nicole muttered.

"I'm telling the story," Brandon said. "So let me tell it my way."

Clearing his throat loudly, Brandon went on. "It was two hundred years ago. The old house next door was the

8

only building in the area except for some small farm-houses. And the old house was much bigger and grander than any of those. It had been built by Captain Elijah Powell and his wife Elizabeth. The captain was a wealthy man, who'd made his fortune from the spice trade."

"The spice trade?" asked Kate, puzzled.

"Yeah," Brandon told her. "You know, like cinnamon and stuff. He sailed around the world to find different spices. Then he brought them back with him and sold them for a lot of money.

"Anyway, they had a baby boy, and he was called Zackary. Now, back then, it took forever to go anywhere by boat. Captain Powell would go off on these long sea voyages that lasted months at a time and leave his wife and son all alone at home.

"He would sail his ship to China and India and places like that. When he got there, he'd get some spices and stuff to bring back with him."

Danny vaguely knew about this. He'd learned a little about it in history.

"Anyway," Brandon said, "one day, he left Elizabeth and Zackary in this big house and sailed off to China for more spices. And he never came back."

Danny stared into the night beyond the tent. It was very dark, with a galaxy of stars visible. He'd never really been able to see the stars in Chicago—there were too many city lights. Out here, it was very different. Sort of unsettling. "What happened to the ship?" he asked.

Brandon shrugged. "It just vanished. Of course, there

9

are plenty of stories. That Captain Powell crossed a powerful witch, or something, and that the witch put a curse on him and his crew. They all died of some horrible disease. Or that a huge storm sprang up at sea and sank the ship. Or that pirates attacked it off the China coast. But there's another story, the one I think is really true.'' He paused, waiting for the inevitable question.

''All right, know-it-all,'' Nicole said. ''Tell us.''

''Some say Captain Powell did something so dark and terrible that he was cursed to wander the oceans forever. And that he can never rest until he's paid for his sins. Somewhere out there at sea at this very moment, his ship is still sailing. It's being whipped by the waves, and driven by insane winds, and the souls of the cursed aboard it are screaming and howling in misery till the end of time.'' His voice faded out to a whisper in the still air.

His listeners shuddered.

''But what about Zackary Powell?'' asked Kate sensibly. ''What happened to Elizabeth and Zackary?''

''Well, she had no way of knowing what happened to her husband,'' Brandon said. ''She kept on hoping that he'd come home. But the months passed, and there was no sign of him. She would go to the docks in town and ask all of the sailors she met if they had news of her husband. And they always told her that they hadn't. But that never stopped her from going down when a ship came in to try and find someone who knew the fate of her lost husband.

''Anyway, the years went by, and the widow Powell and her son grew older. And the money that Captain Powell had left them when he set off for his final journey began to run out. There was the big house to look after, and food and stuff to buy. Then the money was almost all gone, and the widow had to somehow get some cash. Otherwise she and Zackary would starve to death. Zackary was about six or seven when this happened. Anyway, she decided that since the house was so big, she'd make money by renting out some of the rooms.

"Well, at first this was pretty good. There were always sailors who needed a place to stay between sea trips. And there were a lot of people passing through town, which was a really important port back then. It was a hard life, but Elizabeth worked at it. And Zackary helped out as much as he could. So they struggled on for a few years. Then came more bad times. Not enough people wanted rooms, and Mrs. Powell was having to rent for less and less money just to have anyone stay. The house got more and more run-down, because she didn't have the money to keep it up.

"She needed money so bad she couldn't be very picky about who she rented rooms to. One day, two men showed up, an old sailor named Wright, who'd lost an arm at sea, and a creepy-looking man named Gower. Mrs. Powell rented rooms to the men.

"Wright and Gower were really desperate criminals. They were murderers and thieves, and the money they used to pay for their rooms had been pried out of the clenched fist of the last man they'd killed. They had to wash all of the blood off it before they paid Mrs. Powell. But she didn't know that. Anyway, that night in their room, the two robbers laid their plans. They had heard about how Captain Powell had been a trader and how he'd been missing for years. They had also heard gossip that Mrs. Powell had treasure chests of stuff her husband had brought back hidden away that she refused to sell, in case he suddenly came back and needed them. The stories were stupid, because she really was poor. But people believed them. Gower and Wright sure believed them. They figured that the Powell house was stacked up to the attic with hidden treasure. So they decided to rent rooms for the night just to get inside.

"There was only Mrs. Powell and young Zackary in the house with them. So the robbers decided that Wright would take Zackary outside, supposedly to play. Then Gower would make Mrs. Powell tell him where all of her treasure was hidden. So Wright asked Zackary to come outside for a game.

"Meanwhile, inside the house Gower pulled a big, wicked knife from his belt. He grabbed the widow Powell by the hair and held it to her throat. He told her she'd better be quick and show him where the treasure was hidden. 'Cause if she wasn't quick about it, he'd slit her throat from ear to ear." With a leer, Brandon ran his finger around his own throat to show the others how. Kate winced. Danny shook himself to hide a shiver.

Happy with the effect his gruesome tale was having, Brandon continued, "Mrs. Powell told Gower that she didn't have any treasure; otherwise, she'd have sold it to buy food. But Gower didn't want to believe her. He was sure there was gold and diamonds and pearls in the house. When the widow kept insisting there wasn't, he took his knife and . . ." He broke off and lowered his voice. "You don't want to hear what he did. It's not something you forget about in a hurry. But when he was done, Mrs. Powell was a blood-soaked heap, dead on her kitchen floor."

Kate's eyes were wide and frightened. Even Danny felt a little queasy. He wondered if he should insist on all of the gory details. Then he decided he could always ask later. When there was more light.

Brandon was really enjoying himself now. "Well, outside, Zackary could hear his mother's dying screams. He was all set to rush in to try and help her. But one-armed Wright was too fast for him. He grabbed Zackary by the neck in his one hand. Then he lifted Zackary into the air by his neck, and squeezed and squeezed." Brandon's voice sank almost to a whisper. He held out his right hand, and slowly squeezed it into a tight fist.

To everyone's horror, there was a squelchy sort of sound, and then thick, red liquid started to drip from Brandon's fist. Kate screamed, and even Nicole went pale for a second. Danny felt sick.

Then Brandon laughed, and opened his hand. In his palm was a squashed tomato.

"Gotcha," he sneered.

"You're sick, Brandon," Nicole told him. "You know that?"

"Takes one to know one," her brother replied. He wiped off the mess on the grass. "Anyway, after he'd killed Zackary, Wright went to help his partner ransack the house. Naturally, they didn't find anything. So they had killed two people for nothing at all.''

"What happened to them?'' Danny asked, curiously.

"They left town that same night. Nobody knew about it for a few days. Then a sailor came looking for a room to stay. He found Zackary's body down by a little pond behind the house. And inside the house he found the bloody remains of Zack's mother. Soon the news spread that Wright and Gower were wanted for murder.''

Nicole eyed her brother suspiciously. "How did they know that Wright and Gower did it?'' she wanted to know. "The only people who saw them were Zackary and his mother, and both of them were dead.''

"They just knew,'' Brandon replied irritably. "People had seen them going to the Powell house, I guess. And it was how they always worked.''

"Were they ever caught and punished?'' asked Kate in a tiny voice.

"Well, sort of. About a year or so later, they tried to rob another house. But they picked the wrong one, and when they broke in, there was a sea captain just home that day on leave from his ship. He had a gun, and blew out Gower's brains. And then, with his sword, he stabbed Wright in the heart. Both men died instantly.''

There were a few moments of silence after this. Then Danny said, "So where does the haunting come in?''

"It's Zachary,'' Brandon said. "His ghost still haunts the old house. Some people say he's still playing games in the garden. Other people say he's still trying to get back into his house to help his mother. Whatever you believe, his spirit still walks about the grounds. I've seen weird lights in the windows sometimes—spirit lights they're called."

"Fireflies, you mean," said Nicole scornfully.

"Not," Brandon said. "Not on the third floor. It looked like a candle flickering around, or something." He lowered his voice, so the others had to strain to hear him. "And I've been in the yard. There are some spots where if you walk through, it's like someone stabbed you with an icicle. It's all cold and clammy. They say that's where Zackary was murdered. I felt one of them once."

After a short pause, Kate said hopefully, "You're making all this up."

"He is making it all up," Nicole snapped. "He's always lying like that, just to scare people." She glared at her brother. "You're a creep."

"I am not!" Brandon said hotly.

"Look, it's a good story, and it's pretty spooky in places," Danny said placatingly. "But there's no such thing as ghosts and you know it."

"It's true!" Brandon insisted. "Ask anyone."

"Good night, Brandon," Nicole said pointedly.

Danny could see that Brandon was getting mad now.

"I'll tell you what," Brandon said. "If you *really* don't believe that the old house is haunted, let's go over there tomorrow and play, okay?"

Danny knew what he *wanted* to say. He wanted to say, No way! Instead, what he said was: "All right. You're on."

15

"Don't listen to him, Danny," Nicole told him, making a face at her brother. "He's always telling stories. And they're never true."

"This one is," Brandon said flatly. "And, anyway, you'll find out—tomorrow."

Nicole just snorted and rolled over in her sleeping bag.

Kate looked worried and a little sad. "I feel sorry for Zackary," she said thoughtfully. "He was so little when he died."

Brandon gave her a funny look. "Get real," he told her. "He's been dead for hundreds of years. He's a ghost. A spook. You can't feel sorry for a ghost."

"I do," Kate said. "If there really is a ghost, and it's Zackary Powell, he must be terribly, terribly sad."

Brandon stared at Danny. "Your sister's weird," he muttered. "Feeling sorry for a spook!"

As they settled down to sleep, Danny hoped he wouldn't have bad dreams. He took a last look at the house next door, but it was too dark to see anything. At least there were no signs of the funny lights that Brandon had mentioned. But Brandon had to be making it all up. How else would he know all those details? He couldn't know—no one could. It was just a big lie.

Danny didn't really believe that there were such things as ghosts. But . . . for some reason Brandon's story had seemed so real. Maybe Brandon had made some of it up, and some was true? And it had all happened right next door. The old house was standing on blood-stained ground. It made him shiver to think that a kid his age had been brutally murdered there.

Then he pulled himself together. That had been hundreds of years ago—if it had even happened at all. It didn't mean anything right now. It was just a dumb story. There weren't any such things as ghosts. There *weren't*.

All he had to do was to believe that.

THE COLD SPOT

Danny had a bad night. Tossing and turning in his sleep, he kept seeing grotesque images of a one-armed man reaching for him. And feeling something close about his throat, choking him. And there was the face of a young boy. A face with freckles and straw-colored hair. Then the one-armed man came back, a dark, chilling look in his eyes. He had long, dirty hair, and his face was twisted in a snarl. His one arm was huge and heavily muscled. He strode toward Danny, arm raised, fist clenching over and over. And someone calling, calling . . .

Shuddering, Danny rolled over and woke up, his heart pounding.

He lay there in the darkness. He could hear the even breathing of the others and the sound of crickets. That was all. He could have sworn he'd heard someone calling his name. He listened, hardly daring to breathe, but he heard nothing else. It must have just been in the dream.

He felt weird, like there was a giant fist in his chest, squeezing the breath out of him. And there was a strange kind of shiver in his mind. Eventually, though, he calmed down and drifted off to sleep again. In his dreams, the one-armed man was running after him again, this time through a boarded-up old house.

He woke again to the bright sunlight of another perfect morning.

Once they'd washed and dressed and were outside again, Brandon took charge. "You called me a liar last night," he said, looking at all of them. "It's time to put up or shut up. Let's go over to the old house now, and see what we can find."

Danny felt a sort of twisting in his stomach. He had a feeling this was a bad idea. "I'm not sure we should," he said.

"Is little baby Danny too scared?" Brandon jeered.

"No," Danny lied. In fact he *was* scared, even if he didn't know why. It wasn't because of Brandon's ghost story. It was because of his dreams. But he couldn't tell anyone else about them or he'd be laughed at. "But if that place has been empty since Zack died, isn't it kind of dangerous?"

"Like I said, don't believe everything Brandon tells you," Nicole said. "Plenty of people have lived there over the years. It's only been empty like that for about ten years, I think."

"There's more to it than that," Brandon said. "Bad things happened to everyone who ever lived there. After the last one, nobody wanted to buy the place. He was an old guy, threw himself off the cliff. They had to scrape him off the rocks.''

Kate frowned. "Maybe *he's* the ghost haunting the house then?''

"No way,'' replied Brandon. "Everyone knows it's Zack. Anyway, are you coming? Or are you chicken, too?''

Kate pulled herself up to her full height. "I'm braver than *you* are. I'll come.''

"Right,'' Brandon agreed. "Nick-Nack, see if Adam and Tracy want to come, too, okay?''

Nicole wrinkled her nose. The nickname grated on her as always. Then she rolled her eyes. "Okay, I'll go see.''

"We'll meet you there,'' Brandon said. He turned to Kate and Danny. "Come on.''

Danny was feeling very strange about the whole thing. Not scared—well, not *really* scared. More like worried. He wasn't sure why he was so bothered. He was almost convinced that Brandon had made up the whole story just to spook them, and that he was just up to some silly game this morning. But he couldn't forget the bad dreams he'd had. And he had a funny feeling that something weird was going on.

He wished that there was some way he could back out without looking like a dweeb. If only he'd woken up sick or broken his leg or had to go somewhere with his parents! But there was no excuse he could think of. And he couldn't admit that he had a bad feeling about the whole thing. Brandon would only jeer and call him names.

So, dragging his feet every inch of the way, Danny

followed along. He was feeling that this was a big mistake, but he went. Every step he took was like walking through mud. Something seemed to be dragging him back to the peace and safety of his cousins' house. But what? He looked at his sister and Brandon. Even Kate—nervous, chicken-hearted Kate—seemed excited. Normally he'd feel the same way, full of happy, nervous exhilaration at their daring. So why was he feeling like this? Why had Brandon's story gotten to him so badly?

Even though the old house was right next door they couldn't just climb over. The fence around their house was a little too tall. Plus, they were not allowed to climb it and they were in full view of the house. Better safe than sorry. So they had to go around, via the street. There was an old rusting chain link fence around the Powell house, but it had been put up ages ago. There were gaps in the chain links. The gate was chained and padlocked shut, but over the years one of the hinges had broken, and it now hung at a funny angle.

As they stood by the gate, Brandon suddenly leaned on one part of it. With a loud creak, the gate swung free. Kate gave a sharp squeal—half-fear, half-delight. Danny jumped, and Brandon laughed.

"Gets 'em every time," he said.

"How did you know about that?" asked Kate, impressed.

Brandon shrugged. "I told you I'd been in here before." Then he grinned. "I'm not afraid of ghosts!"

"Me either," Kate said.

"So—who's first?" Brandon asked.

21

"You are," replied Kate. "You're talking so big."

"*No problemo*," Brandon agreed. He ducked and clambered through. Holding the gate, he looked back. "Next."

Danny couldn't let his sister go first. It would look bad. So he slipped through and held the gate for Kate to join them.

The old house was large, but it was a mess. The windows and doors were boarded over, and the paint was peeling away. The windows looked like they had all started out with shutters, but many were hanging loose or missing completely. You could still see the faded places where they'd hung. The third-floor balcony had planks missing, and one jagged one had broken. The porch was half-rotted through, and there were holes in some of the walls. The house seemed to be so miserable and sad. Like it was lonely or something. With a shudder, Danny broke out of his mood.

The property was really big. The house was set way back from the road, and the grounds spread out behind it and to both sides quite a ways. The grass was all overgrown, broken here and there by small, tangled bushes.

There was a shout from the street, and Nicole came charging over. Tracy and Adam were on her heels. Kate smiled when she saw Tracy. "Brandon told us this house is haunted."

Tracy laughed. "Everybody tells that old story," she said. "But there's not really a ghost. It's just a joke."

"It's easy to say that in broad daylight," Brandon said solemnly. "I'd bet you wouldn't be so sure at night."

22

"Grow up," Nicole muttered. "So we're all here. Now what?"

"This place is great for games," Brandon said. "Lots of places to hide." He looked over at the house itself.

Before he could say anything, Nicole said, "I don't think we should go into the house. It's probably dangerous. The floors might collapse or something." She looked at her brother, as if daring him to argue. For once he didn't.

"Okay!" decided Brandon. "I know what we can do." His hand flashed out and slapped Adam on the shoulder. "Tag! You're it!" Then, with a yell, he turned and darted away through the long grass.

That broke up the group. Adam whirled and slapped his sister. "Tag!" he howled, and then shot off in the other direction. As Tracy glared around, Danny, Kate, and Nicole all peeled away in different directions.

"Stinker!" howled Tracy. Then she set off after Kate.

Danny ran off to the right. He slipped into the bushes and wormed through the overgrown tangle of branches. After a moment, he realized he was heading back toward his aunt and uncle's house. It was as if some part of him wanted to get out of these grounds as soon as possible. He could hear the others laughing and tried to shake off his own feelings of doom and gloom. Why was he feeling like this?

The pathway was really overgrown. Danny could believe no one had lived here for ten years. It would take an army with flamethrowers to get through all of this! What a mess!

He heard a far-off yell as Kate managed to tag someone. He was fine over here, away from the others. They'd
never be able to tag him. But, just to be on the safe side,
he decided to go just a little further into the bushes.
Luckily, they weren't the sort with spikes or needles or
barbs. Just soft leaves, and tiny twigs.

It was very still here, and almost silent. There was just
the swishing of the branches as he pushed them aside and
the soft sound of his sneakers on the grass. He was
around by the side of the old house now, and his foot
landed on something that snapped under his weight.

Puzzled, he looked down. He'd broken a piece of old
wood. Kneeling down, he realized that it was from some
sort of small fence that had run along this part of the
house—a fence just a foot or so high. What had it been
put here for? As he looked around for some sort of clue,
he suddenly realized what it was.

There was an almost-wild tomato plant there. And a
couple of others. At one time, this must have been a
kitchen garden of some sort. That's what the fence had
been for—to keep rabbits or something out. But the place
was so overgrown now that you couldn't see where the
garden stopped and the vegetable patch began.

Maybe this was something that the widow Powell had
planted two hundred years ago. Trying to grow food that
she couldn't afford to buy, to keep herself and her young
son alive? Danny felt a surge of pity for the long-dead
mother. She must have had a really hard life—losing her
husband at sea, then having to raise her son and take in
boarders. And for it all to end in her being killed by two

heartless thieves. It was sad, even if it was just ancient history.

Danny wandered on, around the edge of the kitchen garden. For some reason, he didn't want to go through that patch. It wouldn't be right to trample on things Mrs. Powell had worked on so hard. There seemed to be another sort of path through here, one that was much easier to walk on.

That was odd. The rest of the place—even the paths— were really overgrown. Why was this one so different? Danny knelt down to look and saw that there was no grass here at all. The soil was dead and packed tight. Maybe there *was* some animal living here after all, and this was a pathway it followed. Maybe it had worn down the grass. But the grass wasn't worn down here—there *wasn't* any grass.

It was like the plants couldn't live on this part of the ground.

And then it struck him. For the past week, he'd been fighting off mosquitoes. They seemed to have a grudge against him. His skin was full of bumps and sore spots. But since he'd come into this garden, he hadn't even heard a mosquito, let alone been bitten.

He stared all around. Weird. In a place as overgrown as this, you'd expect to see some signs of life. Rats or mice, maybe. Squirrels. And birds . . . He looked at the huge trees. There were no signs of nests in any of them. There weren't any birds. He couldn't even hear birds singing. He looked up at the sky. The only shapes he could see were flying far away.

25

It was like all the animals were avoiding this house. He felt a chill in his spine. That was crazy! Animals didn't do things like that. Anyway, there *had* to be bugs and things around. He stared into the grass, but there was no sign of ants or crickets, around him no bees or flies. No nothing.

This was getting really freaky. He'd never heard of any garden without some sort of bugs. His eyes fell on a largish flat rock, and he grinned. Now he could prove all of his worries were just dumb. If you turned a rock over, there were always bugs under it! Those little things with loads of legs that squirmed back into the dark soil. Sometimes centipedes and shiny beetles. He gripped the edge of the stone, then jerked it free and sent it rolling.

Nothing. No pill-like bugs. No beetles. No worms. Just dark, smelly soil . . .

Feeling just a bit more scared and edgy, Danny straightened up. He looked back down the path. It led directly to what had been the back door of the house and seemed to be as straight as if it had been drawn with a ruler. He glanced the other way and saw that the path ended just a few feet farther on, in a circular sort of patch of soil.

Maybe there was a hole there, where whatever had made this path lived? Determined to prove or disprove his fears, Danny slowly walked forward. He tried to convince himself that it was because he didn't want to frighten off any animal that might be there. But he had to be honest and admit that it was really because he suddenly felt very afraid.

Of a path? he jeered at himself.

Of a path where nothing—not even grass—lives, he

answered that part of his mind. What could cause that? Well, what *animal* could?

Then he reached the end of the trail. One last step, and he would be there. He felt an odd reluctance to take that last step. His heart was beating like crazy, and he could hear the pulse over and over in his ears.

This is silly! he told himself. *There's nothing to be scared of. Nothing.*

Liar! said another part of his mind.

He took the step.

As soon as his foot touched the dead earth, it was as if he'd suddenly walked full-tilt into the open door of a freezer. The air felt fifty degrees colder, and his body instantly became frozen on the spot. Jagged waves of coldness washed over him, like icicles being hammered into his body. His breath seemed to chill in his lungs, and he couldn't breathe at all.

He was trapped where he stood, in a dead zone.

27

Chapter Four

THE PAINTING

His heart was pounding, but that was about the only part of Danny's body still working. He couldn't move an inch. Or a muscle. It was as if he were dead, but still in his body. Nothing moved, nothing worked—but he was still there, stuck in place. He couldn't breathe in or out. His head was starting to swim.

A hand suddenly dropped on his shoulder. "Tag!" Tracy yelled in his ear. Then she gave a startled yelp.

And everything began to work again for Danny.

He staggered forward, almost falling before he caught his balance. He was up to his knees in the tall grasses. His breathing had started again, and he was gulping in wild, deep breaths. His head was still spinning, but he could begin to think clearly once more.

"What's with you?" Tracy yelled, rubbing her hand. "You're freezing—like a block of ice! Yuck!"

Danny tried to talk, but at first he couldn't say anything. His voice wouldn't work. Then he managed a croaky sort of reply. "I don't know," he gasped. "It was weird."

"*You're* weird," Tracy shot back. "And you're *it.*" She turned to run.

To his relief, nothing else happened. Danny was almost back to normal now. That chill was still in his bones, though, and even though it was a bright summer day, he wished he had warmer clothes on. He didn't really think that would work, though. This coldness was *inside* him, not outside.

What had happened to him? What *would* have happened to him if Tracy hadn't somehow broken him out of that frozen grip of death? Would he have died where he had been standing? Would the others have found him there, frozen to death, like an icy statue?

Brandon had mentioned something last night about there being cold spots in the grounds. But he'd only been making up that story, hadn't he? Maybe he'd better check with Brandon about this. If Brandon hadn't made it all up, then there really was something very spooky going on here. Danny looked around, but there didn't seem to be anyone near. But what was he expecting to see? One of the other kids? Or a ghost? Danny wished he could just forget that last thought, but it wouldn't go away.

What had happened to him? He'd heard about cold spots in other ghost stories. But they were just supposed to be locations that felt colder than normal—he'd never heard about anyone almost freezing solid in a cold spot. Why him?

Because he'd been on that path? And followed it to the end?

Maybe this house really was haunted, after all?

But he hadn't felt like there was anyone there. And he certainly hadn't seen a ghost or anything. Just that terrible, terrible coldness.

Weird . . .

Danny decided he'd had enough of this place. He turned, got his bearings, and ran back to the break in the fence where they had entered the grounds. Nothing happened on the way, and he didn't stop till he was in the street again. Then he paused. The others would think he was scared, and they'd make fun of him. That almost made him return. Only the chilling memory of what had happened kept him from going back. Well, why should he care what they thought? Let them believe what they wanted. They'd get tired, sooner or later, and leave him alone. But he simply *had* to get out of that terrible garden.

"I give up!" he yelled. "You win!" Was he shouting to the other players? Or to the house? Or to something else? He wasn't sure—and he wasn't going to try and figure it out.

He waited for some sort of response. Again, from whom? Then Brandon and Adam came out of the bushes, scowls on their faces.

"You can't call off the game just like that," Brandon complained.

"Well, I'm not playing in there anymore," Danny said defiantly.

"Scared?" jeered Brandon. Danny might have known. Brandon loved picking on people.

"No," he lied. He considered telling them what he had felt. Then he decided against it. They'd never believe him. They'd think he was making it up to excuse his cowardice. Maybe he could casually mention it to Brandon when they were on their own. Without an audience to play up to, Brandon could be okay. "But that place is too overgrown. There're probably ticks and stuff. We need somewhere better to play."

"Sure," Brandon scoffed. The girls had emerged by now. Kate had grass stains on her knees.

"You're just quitting 'cause I tagged you last," Tracy sneered.

"Think what you want," answered Danny. "I couldn't care less." Then he turned his back on them and marched away.

In a couple of minutes, they had all joined him in the street. It was almost as if they were secretly relieved. Nobody could accuse *them* of being frightened! No way! It was *Danny* who was the wimp.

At least I'm a live, breathing wimp, he told himself.

In a quieter mood, they all returned to the house. The girls went off somewhere to do who-knew-what. Brandon and Adam started a babyish sword fight with sticks. Danny just sat on the porch, shivering and trying to get rid of that chill inside of him.

After lunch, Aunt Sandy announced that she was going into town to do some shopping. "You kids eat more food than a pack of hyenas," she said. "Anyone want to come

31

and help?'' There was dead silence to her offer. "Well, now I know one thing that'll shut you up. Okay, anyone want to look in the game store next to the Food Mart while I shop?'' There was the expected chorus of agreement from all except Danny. He was still finishing his sandwich, still trying to get warm.

But when Aunt Sandy pulled the mini-van out of the garage, Danny went along with the others. He sat in the back, not saying anything. He was still deep inside himself when they arrived at the shopping center in the main part of town.

The others were all eager to head into the game store. They'd counted their money over and over in the van, trying to figure out what they could spend. Brandon seemed to be holding out for a new Nintendo game, while Nicole was insisting on croquet.

Aunt Sandy shot him a concerned look. "Are you feeling okay, Danny?'' she asked.

"Sure,'' he said, quietly. "I just don't feel like shopping.''

"You and me both, kiddo,'' she said with a smile. "It's a dirty job, but someone's gotta do it. You want to stay in the van?''

"No,'' he said, slowly. A half-idea had formed in his mind. What he wanted most of all right now was some kind of an explanation for what had happened to him. And there was one place nearby where he might get some help. "Brandon said that there was a museum in town.''

"The Historical Society?'' When Danny nodded, she

raised her eyebrows in surprise. "It's just a block away," she told him. "Don't tell me you'd rather go there than the game store."

"Yeah," Danny replied. "I'm sort of . . . interested in history."

"I'm impressed," she said, but she looked a little suspicious. Like she *wanted* to believe that was where he was going, but half-expected a trick. "I've always had to drag the kids in there in the past. I'll show you where it is." She led him down the block until they reached an old brick-faced house set back from the road. On the door was the sign:

> BREEDON HISTORICAL SOCIETY
> Museum And Library
> MON–FRI, 9:30–4

"Here you go," Aunt Sandy said. "When you're through, you know where we all are. Okay?"

"Sure," he agreed. He waited until she had started back, then he went up to the door and opened it.

There was a hallway beyond, and an open door at the far end. In between was a small table, where a woman sat reading a soppy-looking novel. She looked up at him. "Hello!" She seemed surprised to see anybody at all.

"Hi," he said awkwardly.

She was old, with wispy gray hair done up in a bun. She gave him a kindly smile. "Feel free to look around. But don't touch anything, please."

"I'll be careful," he promised.

33

"If you've got any questions, do come and ask me. I know most of the answers, and those I don't we can look up together."

He nodded his thanks and then went through the doorway that led to the museum. It wasn't really much of a museum, he saw. There was just the one big room and stairway leading to a balcony above. There were paintings up there and shelves of dusty, uninteresting-looking books. Downstairs in the big room, he found display cases of old photos and artifacts. There were brown pictures of the worst winter on record, in 1902, showing the town all frozen up in ice and snow. There were faded black-and-white pictures of the old whalers and the other ships that had sailed from Breedon.

Danny came upon a row of wooden models of the old ships. They were sort of interesting, especially the warships of 1812. There were dozens of small cannons on those, like in pirate films. Then Danny found a couple of cases of Indian flints and arrowheads that were hundreds of years old and had been dug up all over town. Nearby were cases full of old farm tools and ancient looking plates and glasses and stuff.

There were more bookcases filled with old books. Some had even been written about the town. Danny hadn't realized there was anything about Breedon worth writing about. It seemed like a dull kind of place to him, especially compared to Chicago.

He drifted around the room, poking and not really paying much attention. He really didn't know what he was doing here. It was just a thought that had kind of popped into his head. He regretted passing up the game store.

"Are you looking for anything in particular?" It was the elderly lady again. Had she come to check up on him, or to help?

"I don't know," he told her honestly. Taking a chance, he decided to see what he could find out. "I'm staying with my cousins out on Hill Road, and there's this big old house there."

"Oh, the Captain's place," she said. She grinned mischievously. "I'll bet someone's told you that old ghost story, right?"

He nodded. "About the murder of Zackary Powell and his mother," he said, in case there was more than one.

"That's it." The woman reached over to a bookshelf and ran her fingers along the spines. "It's supposed to be an authentic ghost there, too. Quite famous, in a silly sort of way. Ah." She pulled out a book. It was written by a William Vande Water and entitled: *Ghosts of Old Maine*. She flipped through the pages, then laid the book down on one of the display cases, open to one of the plates. "I can't let you touch this," she told him. "It's over a hundred years old, and we don't have any more copies. But you can have a look."

Danny did so. The page was split into three pictures. The top one, the largest, showed the old house. It looked in better repair, and the grounds weren't overgrown, so it must have been taken a long time ago. The second showed part of an old-fashioned handbill. The headline TWO BLOODY MURDERS! leaped out at him. The rest of it was too small and blurry to read. The third picture was the worst.

According to the caption, it was a picture of one-armed Wright right after he had been shot to death in a burglary attempt. It wasn't a photograph, though. It looked like an old-fashioned engraving. Wright's eyes were closed, but he looked just like the figure that had chased Danny through his nightmares. Even down to his stringy hair, the stubble on the chin, and the squinty look around one eye. Could this just be coincidence? Danny shuddered.

"He's a wretched-looking sort, isn't he?" the woman said.

"What about Captain Powell?" asked Danny, tearing his eyes away from the gruesome page. "Do you have any pictures of what he looked like?"

"Better than that," his guide told him. "We've got an oil painting. This way." She led him to the stairs and started up. "He was a very rich man in his day, and he had a painting of his family done for the old house just before he set off on his last voyage."

"What happened to him?" Danny wasn't going to believe anything that Brandon had said without some sort of backup. Brandon was a well-known liar.

"His ship was lost at sea," the woman replied. "He just never came back." She saw Danny's eyes widen. "Oh, it's not like he sailed into the Bermuda Triangle or anything like that. Back then, going to sea was very danger-ous. By modern standards, the boats were quite small. A lot of ships were wrecked in storms and along shallow reefs. And he was a trader, traveling in the South China Sea, which was a very bad place then, filled with pirates and other cutthroats. He was a spice trader. In those days spices were very valuable. Yes, it could be a dangerous business, but it paid well if you were good at it. And Captain Powell was very good, until that last voyage. There are plenty of theories, but nobody knows for sure what happened to him. Ah, here we are!''

She stopped in front of a large painting. As far as Danny could tell, it didn't look like the artist was that good. The figures looked funny. But she was treating it like a masterpiece or something.

''There's his ship in the background,'' she explained. ''You couldn't really see it from his house, of course. Artistic license, I suppose. Anyway, that imposing-looking fellow is Captain Powell himself. With him is his young wife, Elizabeth, and their son, Zackary.''

Danny felt really strange as he stared at the painting. Not because of the Captain—he was dressed in a heavy-looking dark suit with an odd-looking hat. And not because of Elizabeth. She had on an enormous puffy pink dress.

It was looking at Zackary that made Danny feel peculiar. He was dressed in fussy-looking old-fashioned clothes and held a small whip and a spinning top in one hand. Danny stared in cold wonder at the face of the boy in the picture.

It was as if he had seen that face before. But he hadn't. He was sure he hadn't. Only . . . those freckles and that straw-colored hair were very familiar from somewhere. Then he remembered his bad dreams. . . .

Zackary Powell looked *exactly* like the face he'd seen in his nightmares last night. A sad and tired face.

The face of a ghost?

watching a cartoon, a sitcom, or a talk show, even while he was actually watching it. It all seemed garbled and disconnected.

Amazingly enough, no one came in and bothered him, which was just as well. None of the kids, who were busy with their new games. And none of the grown-ups, who were all busy in different parts of the house. It was just Danny, alone with his confused thoughts.

Eventually he gave up and went looking for the others. They were playing Nintendo in the den, whooping and hollering as the game progressed. Danny sat down, deep in his worries. After a while, he felt an elbow in his ribs, and Nicole handed him the controls.

"It's your turn," she said. "See if you can top Brandon."

"No one can beat me!" Brandon jeered. "He's dead meat. Buzzard bait!"

Danny tried to concentrate on piloting his tiny plane through the enemy tanks. He fired missiles, dropped bombs, and zipped past blazing buildings. He was truly on autopilot. It all washed over him without making any impact.

All the time, there was a strange whisper in his mind. *Come to me. . . . Come to me. . . .* He couldn't seem to shake it. He felt like invisible claws were closing around his brain, draining away his will. He felt a tug in his heart, pulling him back to the old house. . . . And what? What would happen if he went back?

"You're dead!" Brandon screamed, snatching the controls from his hand for his own turn. "What a feeb! Even

41

Kate can beat you!'' He shoved Danny aside and started another game.

Danny, jerked back to reality, discovered that the whisper had vanished.

Finally, the long day ended. It was time for bed. Danny managed to get ready without thinking about it. He even absentmindedly brushed his teeth twice. Then they were out in the garden again, snug inside their sleeping bags.

Brandon grinned evilly around. ''Want another ghost story?'' he asked.

''No!'' Kate and Nicole chorused loudly.

''Suit yourself,'' he shrugged. Then he glanced down at the grass. ''Do you know how many bugs live in this lawn?'' He grinned at them. ''And how many of them crawl through your hair while you're asleep at night?''

''Gross,'' Nicole sneered back. ''You don't have to worry. Your cooties would scare off any other bugs. And we've had enough of you for one day.'' She pulled down the tent flap.

''Who needs girls?'' muttered Brandon. He rolled over to stare thoughtfully at Danny. ''You okay? You've been acting pretty weird all day.''

''I think so.'' Danny wondered if he could tell Brandon anything that had happened to him during the day. Not too much, he decided. Brandon was really okay under his mocking exterior, but still . . . Talking to Brandon was a good way to make sure everyone knew your business. Still . . .

''Did you *really* ever feel one of those cold spots next door?'' he asked.

His cousin grinned. "You really *were* spooked this morning!" he marveled.

Danny knew Brandon was trying to get him rattled, so he didn't give Brandon a chance to get started. "That story you told us," he said. "Was any of it true?"

"Yeah." Then Brandon shrugged. "The history part, anyway. Lots of people say the ghost is real, too. There *are* funny lights there sometimes. He looked at Danny with a puzzled expression on his face. Almost as if he did care but was trying to hide it. "I've heard about the cold spots, but I never really felt one. Did you?"

Danny shook his head. "It's not that," he answered evasively.

Now that it came down to it, Danny felt strangely reluctant to talk about it with Brandon. This understanding mood Brandon was in couldn't last for long. "But I can't explain what it is."

"You're psycho, that's what it is." Brandon rolled onto his back. "There's no ghost there really, dweeb. Don't let it scare you." He grunted. "Ah, there's no point talking to you tonight."

Danny was pleased that his cousin had reached that conclusion, because he didn't want to talk. He wanted to think. The problem was that he didn't seem to be able to string things together at all. He'd start to concentrate on the painting he'd seen this afternoon. Then he'd suddenly think he heard the wind whistling through ropes and rigging, and the crash of the waves against the wooden side of a boat. Or he'd try and remember what he felt when he was in that icy spot, and he'd see a fresh vegeta-

43

ble garden in front of him, with pumpkins, squash, and tomatoes growing. It was as if he'd seen and heard so much today that it was all jumbled together. None of it made any sense. And Danny couldn't sort it out.

Maybe he was coming down with something. His mom had thought so earlier. She'd felt his forehead and insisted he take a couple of aspirin. He wasn't sure they'd done any good, though.

Finally, dizzy with trying to concentrate, he fell asleep. But that didn't stop the weirdness. If anything, it made it worse.

He felt like he was being sucked down a long, dark tunnel, past shapes and figures that slashed out at him with clawed hands. At the end of the tunnel was a bright, pure white light that blinded him. When he could see again, he was no longer himself.

Somehow—and he didn't know just how he knew it—he was Zackary Powell. And he was dead. He had been dead for two hundred years.

Chapter Six

THE
OTHER SIDE

It was no fun being dead.

Danny knew that he was dreaming, but it didn't help. He was somehow inside Zackary Powell's head. He could feel that Zackary had been dead for ages and ages. And he didn't like it at all.

He was standing in the old house, and it was nighttime. That didn't matter, because he could still see everything perfectly. He couldn't feel anything though. It might be summer or midwinter; there was no feeling of warmth or cold. His feet moved carefully on the floor, but he couldn't feel the floor. He had the idea that his feet were bare, but he didn't know for certain.

At one point, he walked clean through a wall. Except for the fact that he could see it, it was as if the wall simply wasn't there. He didn't feel anything at all.

The house was depressing. There was dust and cob- webs all over. A few pieces of furniture leaned in odd corners; but they were broken and had been for years. A

Zack memory told Danny that the rest had been taken out and sold when the house had been boarded up.

Zack didn't seem to be aware of Danny at all, even though Danny was perfectly aware of Zack. Weird. But at the same time it was sort of exciting. Danny realized that, even if he was dreaming, what was happening was also very real.

This was Danny's big chance to get some answers. Was Zack really a ghost? Was he behind all of the strange stuff Danny had been feeling? Maybe, if Danny could just get Zack thinking about the right sorts of things, Danny could get some answers. The first question was: How much of what Brandon had told him was true? Danny tried gently to get Zack to think about his murder.

Zack—still seemingly unaware of Danny—did just that. He remembered the two men, how evil they looked. The one-armed man had taken Zack outside. Then Zack heard his mother screaming. He tried to get away, but one-arm caught him by the throat. The incredibly strong hand choked and choked, until Zack had stopped feeling pain. He never felt anything again.

Danny felt all of this like an old memory washing over him. He felt a sharp, sorrowing pain for Zack. The poor kid—what a horrible short little life he'd had. And now, this . . . A sad, lost ghost, haunting the house where he'd died. But, somewhere in the back of Zack's mind, there seemed to be something more, something he didn't want to think about. Nothing Danny did teased this stray thought out, so he concentrated now on what Zack wanted to think about.

Zack wanted to leave the old house. He'd been imprisoned there for far too long. He couldn't touch anything; he couldn't feel anything. He could only see and hear. He could see other people having a good time. He could hear children playing. Zack kept close to the old house. He didn't know exactly why. Something always seemed to pull him back whenever he tried to leave. Gently, but with a force that couldn't be denied.

Once Zack had realized that he was dead, he'd been hoping to have some fun for a change. He didn't feel sorry that he was dead. He'd actually sort of passed that part of being human. Where he was now there wasn't any work to do, and he didn't feel hunger or pain.

Almost nobody could see him. From time to time, there'd be a person who could somehow look right where he was. Zack never knew what it was that they saw, but they were always terrified.

The first few times, Zack enjoyed spooking people who could see him. It was sort of fun to be able to do *something*. But the people who *could* see him almost never came back again, so he didn't get much pleasure from that game.

He'd tried a few other things, of course. He'd tried lifting things, but he couldn't hold anything. Not a branch, not a leaf, not a pebble. But he could climb a flight of stairs, which made no sense. He couldn't feel the stairs, and if he wasn't thinking, his foot could go right through the steps. But if he concentrated, he could climb up to the top of the house.

Once, he'd even jumped off. That hadn't done him any

47

good. He'd known he wouldn't be hurt, of course, but he hadn't even fallen. He'd just hung there, in the air. Furious, he'd willed himself to fall, to drop like a stone. He finally moved all right, but only to float gently down to the ground like a feather through still air.

Then, realizing that almost nobody could see him, he played spying games. He watched what people did when they thought they were alone. At first, he was amused—and sometimes a little shocked—at what he saw. But, as with everything, the fun wore off fast. He couldn't join in; he couldn't tell anyone what the people he saw did. He couldn't even embarrass people by letting them know they'd been seen.

What hurt him the most was that he didn't even see any other ghosts. He had sort of expected that there would be lots of other ghosts like himself around, but there weren't. Or, maybe they were, but none of them could see each other? He didn't really know.

Once, Zack had actually seen a girl lured into the house, where she was killed. The murder didn't interest him at all, but he'd hung around, hoping that when the girl was dead, he'd at least be able to see her ghost. But then she'd died, and that was it. There was nothing else to see. Bitter and disappointed, he'd gone away.

Danny felt shocked at this. Through Zack's eyes, he had watched the murder. The girl was only around twelve or so. Someone she knew and trusted had taken a knife and used it to slash her until she died. It was horrible and grisly to watch, but the worst part about it was Zack's reaction. He didn't care about what happened to the girl at all, even though she was in terrible pain, screaming and bleeding. He just watched calmly— coldly, even—waiting to see if her ghost would pop out of her body. When it didn't, Zack had simply walked away. If anything, he was angry at the girl for not having a ghost. Danny was horrified by the lack of compassion in Zack. All Zack seemed interested in was how anything might affect him. He didn't have any feelings for the poor murdered girl at all—except disappointment when her ghost didn't show up.

It was so dull for Zack. The only thing that ever broke his awful boredom was being able to scare somebody from time to time. But Zack couldn't plan on that. It either worked or it didn't.

Then—it had happened!

He couldn't remember how long ago it had been. When day and night both looked alike, it was hard to keep track of time. He was in the house. A fat spider was snaring flies in one of the windows. One of the boards covering it had rotted through and fallen, and a shaft of sunlight lit that corner of the house. The spider had come to the sunny spot to spin its web and lure flies to eat.

Zack was annoyed by this tiny creature. He wasn't afraid of spiders—after all, he was dead, and there was nothing that could hurt him at all. Still, it bothered him that the spider had come into his house, unwanted and uninvited. More out of anger and frustration than anything else, he had put his ghostly fist around the spider and *squeezed*.

There was a sudden spark in his fist, as if a shiver had

passed through him. For the first time in countless years, Zack felt something. He felt the death of the crushed spider. He felt the squishiness on his hand. He felt a shock pass up his arm. It touched his heart, and almost exploded. It touched his mind, and suddenly he was really aware of the room. It was dirty, and it stank. There were pools of water where the rain had leaked in. It wasn't really filled with light, as he saw, but mostly black as the pits of night.

And then—almost instantly—the feeling had passed. The dullness and nothingness came back. So did the feeling of light, and the emptiness within his heart. He couldn't feel the spider at all, or its guts on his hand.

But he could *remember* it! For a moment, just a briefest split second, he had felt alive again!

Alive!

Could it happen again, or was this some freak happening? He had to find out. He *would* find out.

All of this seemed as real to Danny as it had to Zack himself. For a while, Danny had been drawn into the mind of the ghost and had lost himself there. Then, suddenly, Zack was gone. Danny screamed and opened his eyes.

Brandon was sitting beside him. "Danny!" he said, a scared look on his face. "You awake?"

With a heavy sigh, Danny tried to calm down. His heart slowed back to normal. He could feel the sweat begin to cool on his forehead, and he was trembling. "Yeah," he said, though it wasn't really true.

"Man, you scared me," Brandon told him. "You were

tossing and turning and muttering to yourself in your sleep. Then you yelled and went all stiff. I thought you were having a fit, or something.''

''No,'' Danny said quietly. ''It was just a nightmare, that's all.''

Uneasily, Brandon settled back down. It was still pretty dark, but Danny could see the worry in his cousin's eyes. ''If you say so,'' Brandon said warily. ''Just try not to have any more, okay?''

''I'll be fine,'' Danny promised. He, too, lay back. But he couldn't get back to sleep. He lay there until morning, wide awake. He was thinking over his dream. Had it just been a dream? Or had he somehow slipped inside Zack Powell—who died hundreds of years ago? Was there some kind of link across the barrier between life and death? Or was it just his overworked imagination and some spooky stories he'd heard?

If he went back to sleep again, would he meet Zack once more?

He was too scared to sleep after that.

Chapter Seven

THE RESTING PLACE

The next day, Danny was tired and mentally worn out. He practically sleepwalked through breakfast. He put on socks that didn't match, and his sweat shirt was on backward.

Danny wished there was someone he could talk to about everything he'd felt. But all his friends were back in Chicago. Even if they weren't, he wasn't sure he could get anyone to believe him. He knew it wasn't even worth trying to tell his parents or Uncle Bill and Aunt Sandy. It was such an incredible story. Actually, he wondered if *anyone* would understand him. He didn't even understand himself!

He finished his juice, then stacked his breakfast dishes in the dishwasher. Finally, he went outside.

It was another fine day. He wished it would rain, just for a change, but there wasn't a cloud to be seen. Adam and Tracy were over again, and they were talking with Brandon, Nicole, and Kate.

somehow. But the dead boy certainly wasn't here. If he was anywhere, it was back at the old house. *If* you believed in ghosts. Which Danny didn't.

Brandon would laugh himself silly if he knew how badly Danny was spooked! And by a dumb old painting that wasn't even very good. It was nothing, just a case of overactive imagination. Nothing more than that.

Nothing.

He was waiting by the van when Aunt Sandy arrived with the groceries. She seemed surprised to see him and roped him in to helping load the stuff in the back. Then he waited in the van while she went to find Brandon, Nicole, and Kate. Danny spent the time gripping the edge of the plastic seat with taut fingers.

This is real, he told himself, over and over. *This is the 1990s, not the 1790s. Zack is long dead and gone. Ghosts don't exist, and I'm perfectly all right.*

The only problem was that he didn't believe it. No matter how often he repeated it, he couldn't get rid of the feeling that *something*—or *someone*—from the past *was* still around. Not alive, exactly, but around.

The others were excited with what they'd managed to buy at the store, but it all wafted past Danny like so much smoke. Ten seconds after he'd been shown the purchases, there was no way he could have named them. He felt as if the world about him was slowly becoming unglued. As if he were being pulled away from it. Once they got home, he sat in the big kitchen by himself.

Nothing would get rid of this eerie mood. Even watching TV didn't help. He couldn't have said whether he was

"Hey, slowpoke," Brandon said. "We thought you'd decided to clean the house or something. Come on."

"Where to?" he asked.

"Back to the old house," Brandon said casually. "We've still got to finish that game of tag we started yesterday. You're it, remember?"

The old house! Everything inside of Danny wanted to scream out and refuse to return there.

"Okay," he heard himself say. Stunned, he tried to take it back. But he found himself running along with the other five, and nothing he wanted to do seemed possible.

This was way beyond weird now. It was terrifying. It was as if he wasn't in control of his body anymore. And in the background of his mind was that whisper again: *Come to me. . . . Come to me. . . .*

A terrible thought struck him. Maybe his dream *had* somehow been real, and he had managed to enter into Zack Powell's mind. And maybe, now that he was awake, the reverse had happened. What if Zack Powell was inside of him? Making him go back?

They slipped through the broken gate and into the grounds. As the others ran off, laughing, Danny paused. He felt like he was back in control again. Some sort of cloud lifted from his mind. His first instinct was to run, to get away from this place.

The others would think he was a coward, but he didn't care. Let them think what they wanted! The only reason he didn't turn and run was that he was afraid he couldn't do it. If Zack Powell *had* taken him over once, he could probably do it again, and bring him back. No, there was

53

only one way he could get out of here and not come back.

He had to find out what was going on. Was there *really* a ghost here? Or was he imagining the whole thing?

The others had a pretty decent head start by now. Danny set off after them. Today, though, he kept well away from the kitchen garden and the right side of the house. He angled across to the left, trying to be quiet. It wasn't easy when he had to push through bushes and cut across long grass. Still, the others had the same problem. If they could hear him coming, he could hear them going.

After a few moments, he heard movement in the bushes ahead and to the right of him. They were kind of close to the house, and he wasn't sure he wanted to go in that direction. It took all of his courage to dash across and reach into the bushes.

"Tag!" he yelled loudly. He heard Adam yelp, and then Danny took off, putting as much space between him and the house as he could.

He went back and to the left. After a minute or so, he no longer heard Adam trying to chase him. Instead, the dead silence of yesterday fell once more. There were no birds singing, no squirrels chattering and whipping up and down trees, no rabbits munching the grass, no bugs buzzing or crawling. He'd almost forgotten how unsettling this was. Maybe all the animals knew this was a bad place, too. Danny tried to turn and leave but felt that same strange refusal of his body to do what he wanted. As soon as he stopped trying to leave, the feeling passed.

He pushed past a couple of large birch trees, until he reached a sort of hollow in the ground. He could hide out here if he wanted. He'd hear anyone coming a mile away. But he felt too restless to stay here. He kept moving.

At the end of the depression, he stumbled over something. He fell down, and his knee seemed to explode against something hard. He sat down to examine the wound.

He'd skinned his knee pretty badly, and there was blood all over it, mixed with grass and some dirt. He felt in his pocket for a tissue. He found a mostly clean if crumpled one, and pressed it to his knee. It stung, but he kept it in place.

What had he tripped over? A tree root, maybe? He looked back, one hand holding the tissue to his knee. There was something there in the grass all right. It looked gray, almost black, and large.

He brushed aside the grass with his fingers, and then found a small broken branch to finish the job. After a couple of strokes with his wooden brush, he had a pretty good idea of what he'd stumbled over. But he kept going, grimly trying not to think about it. When it was all cleared away, he stared at it.

It was a gravestone. It had fallen backward, and part of the top had broken off. There was a little moss growing in the bottom corner, and the engraving was really battered. There were still some letters that hadn't worn away, and Danny brushed at the surface of the stone, trying to make them out more clearly.

Z–something or other–*K*–something–*R*–

He felt a chill clear through to his bones.

Zackary! This was Zackary Powell's gravestone!

He managed to make out the date 1787, but that was all. With a shudder, he sat back on his heels. He'd literally stumbled over Zackary's grave. The dead boy had been buried right here!

Danny leaped to his feet, realizing with a shiver that he was sitting on the grave itself. Straightening up made his knee hurt, and the blood began to trickle again. Still, the pain in his leg kept him from getting really scared about the whole business. With all of the space to run around in, he'd managed to stumble over Zack's grave.

Coincidence? Maybe Zackary was somehow directing his footsteps?

But this was silly! Even if it *was* his grave, so what? What could he do? He'd been dead for centuries.

Something made Danny look up toward the house. It looked as it always did, except for one third-floor window. The boards were gone, and he could see inside perfectly clearly.

There was a movement in the light, and a figure moved into the frame of the window.

It was Zackary Powell . . . dressed in his funny clothes and staring directly down at the intruder who was standing on his grave.

As he stared back at Zack, mesmerized, Danny suddenly felt a hand on his shoulder. He screamed in terror, and whirled around.

"Tag!" said Brandon. "You're it." Then he saw Danny's face, and his eyes widened. "What's the matter with you?" he asked.

"There," Danny said, grabbing Brandon's shoulder

with one hand, and pointing with the other. "On the third floor. In the window. It's Zackary Powell!"

Brandon looked scared for a minute; then, he looked up. "Right," he agreed, rolling his eyes. "You're just trying to get me back for yesterday, aren't you? That ghost story got to you, and now you're trying to weird me out, right?"

Slowly, afraid of what he would see—or *not* see— Danny turned.

There was no unboarded window. There was no room visible. And there was no figure of Zack. Just the empty, dead house, as usual.

Chapter Eight

THE SECOND DREAM

"Nice try," Brandon told him, with a grin. "For a second there, I thought you'd really seen something. You're good at this stuff, aren't you?"

"I guess," Danny said, with a sigh. There was no point in trying to explain. Then he remembered the gravestone. "Take a look at this," he suggested.

Brandon looked down, then did a double-take. "Cool!" he exclaimed. "A headstone." He knelt down and studied the slab. "Can't make out anything, though."

"It's Zackary Powell's," Danny said. "You can read some of the letters."

"You've either got microscopic vision or you're trying to sucker me again," his cousin said. "You can't make any letters out here at all."

Danny bent closer to look, though he was sure he knew what he'd see. Brandon was right—the stone was much too weathered to read anything at all on it. And there was

58

moss all over it, too. That wasn't how it looked before—
but, again, Brandon would never believe it.

Pain shot through Danny's knee as he straightened up,
and he couldn't keep himself from yelling. Nicole came
running. She ignored Brandon and stared at Danny's
knee. It was still bleeding.

"That looks pretty bad," she said. "We better get
you home." She looked down at the gravestone, and
she didn't seem to see more than Brandon had. "If you
fell on this filthy thing, we'd better put on some antiseptic."

"Right," said Brandon unhelpfully. "Or it might get
moldy, and we'd have to saw it off."

Aunt Sandy took one look at the knee and sent Brandon
for the first aid kit, while she half-dragged Danny into the
upstairs bathroom. Carefully, she bathed his knee with
peroxide while he sat on the edge of the tub. Then she
used tweezers to pick out the bits of embedded dirt and
twigs. It hurt like anything, but Danny managed to clench
his teeth and not make any noise.

Finally, Aunt Sandy slathered antiseptic on and wound
yards of gauze and tape into a sturdy bandage.

"Well, I guess you'd better stay in the rest of the day,"
she told Danny. "Rest your knee—prop it up and watch
some TV."

Being forced to relax improved Danny's spirits a lot.
The strange pull toward the old house seemed to have
vanished now. He didn't feel that whispering in the back
of his mind. His knee stopped hurting, except when he

tried to bend it too far. Aunt Sandy kept checking up on him, which made him feel a little better.

Maybe he could talk to her about Zackary Powell. He badly wanted to talk to someone, and she did seem extra sympathetic right now. After thinking it over for a while, he decided not to risk it.

Danny sat and brooded in the den. There wasn't any point in telling anybody what was going on. Face it, he told himself, *no one* will believe it. Why was the ghost appearing only to him? Did it want something from him? Was he the only one who could see it?

Or was he—just imagining things? Maybe . . . maybe he was losing his mind.

He almost *wanted* to believe that! Anything was better than the idea that he was being personally haunted. But . . . that cold spot hadn't been his imagination. Tracy had felt it, too. Okay, so Brandon hadn't seen either the ghost or the writing on the tombstone. But the stone was real. If only somebody else had seen the ghost; that would settle the matter once and for all.

What if . . . what if one of the others *had* seen it, but like Danny was too afraid of getting laughed at to admit it? The only way he'd find out would be to admit first that he'd seen it. It seemed like a no-win situation.

He fell asleep finally. There was a kind of chilling wrench inside of him, and he felt sick. Then he was inside Zack Powell again as before.

The same strange light from the last dream was back, and he could see all around him as if it was daytime. In fact, it might even have been daytime. There wasn't really

any way for him to tell. The sky was filled with dark, angry clouds, and he couldn't see either the sun or moon. He realized that there was rain falling all around him— and through him. Being a ghost, the rain couldn't touch him or wet him.

He could see it splashing up from the ground, creating huge, muddy puddles. But wherever Zackary walked, it just seemed perfectly dry.

Zackary seemed to have some aim in mind, but Danny couldn't quite make it out. He just paid attention as Zack walked through the rain to the large birch on the front lawn of the old house. It didn't seem to be as overgrown as Danny remembered it, so this must be an old memory. He felt certain that he was reliving something that had happened to Zack in the past—if *reliving* was the right word for the memories of a ghost.

Zack started to climb the tree. He couldn't feel the branches at all, with either his hands or feet. But if he concentrated hard enough, he could climb the tree as if he really did have a solid body. It felt really freaky to Danny.

There in a hollow in the tree trunk was a bird's nest. The mother bird had settled onto her eggs, sheltering them with her wings. It was snug and warm in there, safe from the storm. The bird looked up, seeming to sense Zack. It started to make horrible clicking sounds, and then it reared up, flapping its wings as if to fend him off.

Not worried about this at all, Zack reached out for the bird. His hand passed through the wings without touching anything. Then he *squeezed* and wished that the bird was dead. It was what he had done with the spider in the last dream.

The same electric tingle ran up his arm. The bird gave a dreadful scream and thrashed about for a second. It couldn't break the ghost's grip, though, and it suddenly went limp. It was dead.

The feeling of shock lasted. Zack's heart seemed to race, and his mind almost exploded. The day suddenly turned black once more, and with a shudder he could feel the rain falling on his skin. In a second or two, he was soaked through.

Zack laughed. He turned his face up to the sky, and the stinging rain slapped his skin. His hair was drenched, and his clothes plastered to his soaked body. He could feel the branch under his feet and the trunk he had his arm around.

Zack was alive again!

And then it was gone. The tingly feeling died away. His heart felt fainter. The rain started to fall through him again, and the feeling of wetness slowly wore away. The day became brighter once more, and the tree seemed to lose its solidity.

He was a long-dead ghost once more.

The disappointment was too much for Zackary. He let go of the tree, and drifted back down to the ground. He shook his fist at the sky.

"It's not fair!" he screamed. "It's not fair! It almost worked. I was almost real again!"

Furiously, he turned and ran back toward the old house. There was a dizzy sort of feeling washing over

Danny. Somehow he knew that time was passing. Giddily, he seemed to be watching Zackary's experiences in fast-motion, like when he played the VCR on fast-forward. There were people living in the house, but they seemed unaware of Zack. Then, in a fit of fury, the ghost managed to channel all his rage into an explosion of activity.

Danny watched helplessly. The family had been eating dinner. Suddenly, plates shot like rockets across the room. The cutlery danced over the table and leaped to the floor. The food jerked off the plates, slapping people in the face.

If he'd seen it in a film, Danny would probably have laughed. The dinner was attacking the humans trying to eat it. But the terror that the people felt was so real, so chilling, that Danny wanted to scream out for Zack to stop. But he could do nothing.

Finally the anger passed. As Zack calmed down, the plates crashed to the floor, shattering into millions of fragments. The silverware clattered to a stop, and the food splatted to the floor.

The family fled the house and never came back again. Giddily, Zack seemed to explode into activity, after decades of doing nothing. Danny saw and felt Zack stalk and kill rats and rabbits. Each time, he seemed to become real for a short while, but it always faded away again after a minute or two.

One time, he cornered a cat. The poor creature, its fur bristling like crazy, clawed and spat at Zack. It screeched and howled, but nothing it did could touch the ghost.

Then Zack killed it with his dreadful touch. The feeling of being real lasted almost half an hour after that. And when he went back to being a ghost, it *hurt*. It was almost as if he were dying over again.

That scared Zack. He had not felt pain like that in almost two hundred years. He never wanted to again. Danny had felt the pain as well, like a terrible cold ache through his heart.

Danny wished he could be free of this nightmare, but he couldn't wake up. He was forced to stay in Zack's pain-filled mind. For a while after this last shock Zack had avoided killing things. But the hunger to be real again finally overcame even his fear of the awful pain. He killed another rabbit, but steered clear of anything larger for a while.

Danny now realized why there was no animal life at all in the grounds of the old house. Zack killed anything that did come there. The wildlife must have somehow wised up to the fact that the whole area was deadly. Was that why they kept away?

Danny felt bewildered. Zack didn't seem to care at all about killing things. And it was all for this strange feeling that he was alive again. It never lasted, and Zack knew it. Yet he couldn't seem to stop what he was doing. It was like a drug for Zack, Danny realized. Zack was addicted to being alive.

"It's not fair!" Zackary would scream sometimes. "I never had a real life! I was killed by that robber! He stole my life! I want to live! I want to live!"

Danny could understand that. Zack had been so young

when he had died. It did seem unfair. At the same time, Danny was disgusted and repelled by Zack killing animals for that small taste of life they afforded him.

Danny was feeling more and more light-headed. He was fading out of Zack's mind; he was waking up. The last thing he heard in his dream was Zack: "There must be a way for me to become completely real again. There must be. And I'll find it. I know I will!"

With a shudder, Danny woke up.

CHILD'S PLAY

Danny was finding it harder and harder to concentrate on the normal parts of his life. He forgot completely about breakfast until his mom reminded him.

"It's not like you to miss a chance to eat," she said. "What is it? That knee bothering you?"

He had completely forgotten about his hurt knee. "No," he told her honestly. "It feels fine. I just have a lot to think about."

"Well, never let it be said I stopped you from thinking!" His mother laughed. "But think about food for the moment, okay? How do waffles sound?"

After breakfast, Danny went out in the yard. He kept to himself, avoiding his sister and cousins. He needed to think.

Was there *really* a ghost named Zackary? Or was it all nothing more than his imagination and bad dreams? Brandon hadn't seen the writing on the gravestone or the

66

ghost in the window. When Danny had looked a second time, he hadn't seen them either.

Was his mind playing tricks on him? But what about the vivid memories of Zack's life? Could he have just dreamed them? And that sense of purpose Zack had. Danny couldn't see how that could just be an overactive imagination on his part. Zack seemed to have a plan that had something to do with killing all the animals around the old house. There weren't any animals there at all— that was a fact, not imagination. That, at least, was proof that he wasn't just inventing it all.

Zack's terrible thirst for killing small animals really bothered Danny. At first, Zack had seemed to be almost a sad sort of ghost. Danny had felt sorry for him.

But now . . . Danny didn't feel so bad for the ghost. Zack spent his time killing everything he could so that all the animals stayed away from the old house now. Zack seemed to enjoy that kind of thing, and Danny knew it was a sick sort of person inside who'd kill all those animals. In fact, in his dreams, he'd felt unclean when he was in Zack's thoughts then.

Danny remembered some of the things Zack had done when he knew he couldn't be seen. He'd watched that poor girl being killed, for instance, and not even felt sorry for her. How could anyone not have felt bad about that? What kind of a person was Zack?

Maybe this was why he was so alone? Because even the ghosts of the other dead people didn't want to have anything to do with him. Danny wouldn't blame them. Brandon was a pain at times, but he wasn't cruel or cold like Zack. Maybe Zack hadn't always been like this, but now he seemed to be some kind of horrible bully that enjoyed what he did.

Danny was certain that the best thing he could do would be to stay away from the old house. Zack, for some reason, didn't seem to be able to go very far from it himself. So if Danny stayed away, then he'd be safe from Zack.

There! He'd put his finger on the uneasy part of his thoughts. *Safe* from Zack.

He had a bad feeling that Zack had something ugly in mind for him. Danny wasn't sure what it could be, but he felt convinced Zack was up to no good. Going to the old house again was completely out of the question.

Brandon walked over. "Yo, Earth to Danny. Wake up. Adam and Tracy are here. You wanna go play tag next door again?"

No way! was what Danny meant to say. But, once again, he seemed unable to say it. "Okay," he heard himself agree. He tried to get together the mental energy to stop himself from moving. But he stood up, and ran to the old house's fence again. Once more he could feel the force of that whispery voice calling to him. It had to be Zack. But how? And why?

Once inside the fence, Danny felt the compulsion fading, and his first thought was to turn and run for it. But, as before, his feet wouldn't obey. Brandon grinned and slapped Tracy. "Tag! You're it!" Then, laughing, he ran off.

Maybe he could ruin the game, Danny thought. Stand

still, let Nicole tag him, and then refuse to play? But his feet—so unwilling to move a moment ago—seemed to have made up their own minds. He found himself running away from Nicole as fast as his rebellious legs could carry him. It wasn't until he was in the bushes by the side of the house that he regained control and could slow down.

These crazy fits were scaring him. How could he lose control of himself like this? Was it some mental sickness? Or was it Zackary Powell somehow controlling his actions? Either way, he was very afraid. How could he stay away from Zack when he couldn't control his body?

He could hear the others laughing. Tracy must have managed to tag someone, and the game was going full-speed now. He was out of the way here, down by the side of the house again. It was the side where the gravestone lay. He didn't want to get too close to that again, but neither did he want to get closer to the old house than he had to. That was where Zack usually seemed to hang around. He veered farther outward, trying to circle around the grave.

Looking back, he could just make out one of the girls running pretty close to the side of the house. From the flash of yellow hair, it had to be Tracy. She must be going around the back of the house, avoiding as much of the undergrowth as she could.

Well, she was probably safe enough. Zack was after him, not her. Danny kept on moving, but his attention was drawn back to the house. This time, he saw another of the girls close to it. Nicole, judging from her size. She wasn't running, but trotting, looking all around. She was obviously it, and looking for someone else to tag. She probably wasn't looking for him to be this far away, so he crouched down, and peered back at her through the branches of a shrub.

Nicole had almost reached one of the windows on the side of the house. She wasn't looking toward the house, naturally, since she knew it was boarded up. But from where he was hiding, Danny could see it perfectly.

The boarded-over window blinked out, suddenly. It was open again, and he could see the room beyond. And, in the window, Zack Powell. On his face was a twisted sort of smile. Danny caught his breath and felt his heart pounding. Nicole hadn't seen him, of course. With a nasty expression of happiness on his face, Zack walked through the window and wall of the house. Then he reached out his hand toward Nicole.

Danny knew at that instant what Zack was planning—it was how he had killed those animals! He had reached out and *squeezed*—and he was reaching for Nicole!

Jumping to his feet, Danny screamed out Nicole's name and waved his hands hard. She looked up, startled, and puzzled. He was supposed to be hiding, not showing himself. Was this a trick? Danny could see all these thoughts pass through her mind. And while she stood there, Zack was getting closer to her.

"Run, you jerk!" he yelled.

"I'm gonna get you, Danny Walker!" Nicole threatened. She started toward him, but it was too late. Zack had reached her.

The grin on the ghost's face was twisted now, and he shot his hand out—straight into Nicole. She gave a sudden cry of shock, and went stiff. Zack stood there, his fist buried inside her, squeezing and grinning like crazy.

Fear and anger filled Danny, and he didn't stop to think. He ran as fast and hard as he could across the tangled space toward his cousin. She seemed to be frozen to the spot, just as he had been on the other side of the house. Had Zack done this to him there? Was this the explanation for the cold spot? It had to be!

Danny was desperately afraid he'd be too late to stop the ghost. Heart beating crazily, he ran as fast as he could, jumping and dodging everything in the way. Could he save Nicole? His eyes wouldn't focus properly, and his breath was sawing in his throat, hurting him with every gasp.

Then he was there, and he threw himself at Nicole. His weight sent her tumbling backward. They both fell right through the grinning ghost of Zack Powell. A momentary chill shot through Danny as he passed through Zack. Then it was gone.

Nicole gave a huge shudder, then seemed to be waking up as if from sleep. She blinked, and Danny could hear her taking huge ragged gulping breaths. Her arm was stone-cold where he held it, and she started to shiver from the coldness in her bones. It was exactly how Danny himself had felt.

''What . . . what?'' she tried to say, but her teeth were chattering too much for her to manage more than that.

Then she went stiff again and gripped his wrist. Her

fingers were like icicles closing on his flesh. With her other, shaking, hand she pointed over his shoulder.

"Can . . . can you see that?" she asked.

Danny glanced over his shoulder, and saw Zack watching them. The ghost's eyes were full of amusement and something else. Scorn?

"Yeah," Danny told his cousin. "That's Zackary Powell."

"You can see him, too?" she asked in a frightened voice. "Right through him? He's really a ghost?"

"Oh, yeah." Danny looked at Zack again, who hadn't moved. What was he up to? Why hadn't he attacked Danny or Nicole again? Danny shifted around, so he could help his cousin and still keep an eye on Zack.

"How brave you are," Zack sneered. It was the first time he'd ever spoken directly to Danny, and Danny was astonished to hear a voice. It was thin and reedy, like the wind. But the words were quite clear. Nicole clutched Danny's arm tighter. She could obviously hear Zack, too. Zack spoke again. "Coming to help your cousin like that." He didn't sound impressed.

"Danny," Nicole hissed, white showing around her wide eyes, "he's talking to us!"

"He's after something," Danny told her. "I don't know what, but he seems to want us around for some reason."

"Did you really think I'd kill her?" asked Zack. He took a ghostly step, and Nicole gave a little shriek. Zack pulled a face at her and then laughed when she clutched Danny. "I'd forgotten how frightened people can get."

"Make him go away," Nicole begged Danny. "Please—I'm scared!"

"So am I," Danny told her. "But I don't know *how* to make him go away."

"No," agreed Zack, happily. "You can't even keep away from me, can you? And I can do anything I want. Anything at all. You can't stop me, Danny. In fact, you're going to help me."

"I wouldn't help you for anything," Danny said, angrily. "You're wicked . . . evil."

Zack didn't seem bothered by this. "Takes one to know one," he said, laughing.

Nicole was scared, but she seemed to be trying to make sense of what was happening. "He's not talking like a ghost," she whispered to Danny. "He sounds so . . . *modern*."

Zack laughed again. "Hey, I may be *dead*, but I can still learn. I've been watching and listening to people. You'll do. You'll do whatever I want. Or else . . ." He let his voice trail away menacingly, and then he turned around and ran back through the wall of the house.

As soon as he'd gone, Nicole jumped to her feet. The skin where Danny was touching her arm was almost back to its normal temperature again. "Let's get out of here!" she snapped. "Before he comes back!" Before either of them could move, though, they heard two sounds.

The first was a loud cracking noise, like wood breaking.

The second was Tracy screaming like a trapped animal.

TRACY
IN TROUBLE

Danny and Nicole stared at each other. Danny could see she was thinking the same thing he was: *Zackary had done something to Tracy!*

Nicole couldn't run fast. She was still too weak. Danny was still tired from his last run, but he went as fast as he could. His legs ached, and his chest felt like it was on fire. But he kept going and came around to the back of the house.

He managed to stagger to a halt just in time.

The ground had opened up in front of him, and there was a gaping hole. He realized that it wasn't the earth that had given way, but some old planking. It had splintered and collapsed under Tracy's weight. Was Tracy hurt? Or even . . . worse?

"Tracy!" he yelled, getting as close as he dared. He saw that a layer of earth and grass had covered the planks. She hadn't even seen them in her path.

"Danny?" Her voice came up, weak and terrified. "Is that you?"

"I'm here," he called down to her. "Are you okay?"

"I . . . I think so. My ankle hurts. I fell on it." Her voice quavered. "Danny, I'm *scared*. Get me out of here!"

"Okay," he said. "We'll do it. How far down are you?"

"I can see the hole I fell through," she told him. "I guess it's about ten feet above me."

"Okay. Just stay still."

"Okay. It's like a pond, or something, down here. I'm wet and it's all muddy," Tracy told him.

Danny could hear Nicole not far behind him, howling at the top of her voice for the others. "Stay cool," he told Tracy. "We'll get you out. But we need rope or a ladder or something."

"Don't go away!" she said, frightened. "I don't want to be all alone."

At that moment, Brandon came tearing around the house, and skidded to a halt. He took the scene in at a glance.

"Jeez," he muttered. "She must have fallen into the old pond. It's been boarded over for years."

"We've got to get her out," Danny yelled at him. He couldn't believe Brandon was so calm.

Brandon just shook his head. "We'll never manage it," he said flatly.

Danny felt like killing him. "Look," he suggested. "Go home, and tell your mom what happened."

"You kidding? She'll kill us!"

Danny pointed at the hole. "We need help to get Tracy

75

out of there. Go home, and tell your mom. We need a ladder or rope or something. And hurry up about it.''

Without another word, Brandon turned and dashed away. Danny bent back as close as he dared to the hole. It was pitch-black down there, and he couldn't see a thing.

''Take it easy,'' he told Tracy. ''Brandon's gone for help, and I'm still here. You'll be out of there in no time. Trust me.''

''All right,'' agreed Tracy. She sounded a little calmer. ''I'll be okay.''

''It won't be for long,'' Danny promised her. ''Just hang in there.''

Nicole came around the corner of the house, Adam and Kate on her heels.

''Is Tracy okay?'' she asked. Her voice was raspy, but strong. Danny nodded.

Adam shook his head in wonder. ''What a klutz,'' he muttered, eyeing the hole that held his sister.

A few minutes later, they all heard sounds from the front of the house. Brandon dashed around the corner. ''Mom's coming, and so is Mr. McCall. They've got a ladder and rope.'' He skidded to a halt. ''Some excitement, huh?''

The two adults arrived seconds later. Mr. McCall looked almost gray with worry. He ran over, carrying a tall ladder on one shoulder, and leaned as close to the hole as he dared.

''Tracy!'' he yelled. ''Are you okay?''

''Daddy!'' she called back. ''I'm okay, but my ankle hurts.''

"I don't know what possessed you kids to play here," Mr. McCall muttered. Danny didn't say what he thought: *Possessed* was probably the right word to choose. As Aunt Sandy arrived carrying a rope, Mr. McCall shook his head.

"I'm afraid to move any closer. That wood looks rotten to me. If I step on it, I could bring the whole thing down on Tracy."

"I could do it," Danny volunteered. He needed to do something.

Mr. McCall looked at him thoughtfully. "My wife's called the fire department," he replied. "We could wait till they get here."

"Don't leave me down here!" begged Tracy.

Her father sighed. "Okay," he said to Danny. He dropped the ladder and took the rope from Aunt Sandy. "I'll hang onto you. If it looks like you're going through, I'll pull you back." He fastened the rope around Danny's chest, under his arms. "Take it nice and easy," he advised.

"Right." Danny was more than willing to follow that advice! He had no desire to go crashing through to join Tracy. Carefully, he stepped forward. He was still on solid ground. Another step. And another. With that one, he could feel a difference under his sneaker. "Here's where the planks begin," he said.

"Easy," Mr. McCall advised him.

Danny inched out. The boards creaked a little, but they didn't seem ready to splinter. Slowly, carefully, Danny brought his other foot up until he was standing with all of his weight on the wood. He didn't fall, though he could feel the wood sagging a bit. Another couple of steps should do it. Completely focused on what he was doing, he took a second step and then the third. He was on the edge of the hole now. He could smell something rank below.

"Okay," he said. "I think I can guide the ladder down now."

Mr. McCall nodded to Aunt Sandy. She and Brandon grabbed the ladder, and swung the end around to Danny. He started to crouch down, very slowly. The boards creaked dangerously, but they still held his weight. It was like balancing on a trampoline.

Grabbing the first rung of the ladder, he guided it into the hole.

"I can see it!" Tracy yelled up. "It's right above me."

"Okay, baby, okay," her father replied. "Watch it, now. Try to stay out of the way as it comes down."

Danny fed the ladder down more and more. It was getting heavier and harder for him to control.

"We've got to let go now," Aunt Sandy told him. "It's going to be heavy. Will you be okay?"

"I think so," he told them. It was hard, but finally the ladder was all the way down. Danny breathed a sigh of relief. "Can you climb out?" he called down to Tracy.

There was a pause. Then Tracy cried out. "I don't think so," she said shakily. "My ankle kind of hurts. I can't climb properly."

Danny looked uncertainly into the darkness below. "I guess I'll go down," he said, finally. "If I tie the rope around Tracy, you could pull her out."

"You'd have to wait in the pit till she's out," Mr. McCall said. "That rotten wood won't hold both of you at once."

Danny looked into the smelly hole again. Swallowing, he nodded. "I'll be okay," he said uncertainly. Carefully, he climbed onto the ladder. Slowly, carefully, he edged his way down the rungs and into the blackness.

He could hear Tracy's breathing—short and nervous. She was really scared. He couldn't blame her for that. "Hold on," he called down. "I'll be with you in a minute."

"Okay." Her voice was barely more than a whisper.

Finally, he reached the bottom. He could just make out Tracy in the dim light from above. Carefully he untied the rope around his chest. Then he helped Tracy tie it under her own arms.

"Okay!" he yelled. "She's coming up now!"

"Right," he heard her father call back. "Come on, honey—we'll pull. That'll help."

Tracy took a step onto the ladder, whimpering at the pain in her injured ankle. Danny helped her. Screwing up her strength, she gingerly kept going. The rope kept her from having to put too much weight on her bad ankle.

Danny watched her climb slowly up the ladder. He'd be down here on his own until she was up. He didn't like the idea much, but at least he wasn't hurt. He looked around. The light was bad—and so was the smell—but he could make out a few things in the hole. It had been some sort of pond once, as Brandon had mentioned. It must have been a long time ago, though. There were some old stones lining the pit, all overgrown with things that Danny didn't want to look closer at. And the ground was uneven, mostly mud and rocks.

Something in the mud caught Danny's eye. It looked like a piece of wood. Danny kicked at it, but it seemed stuck in the mud.

Well, there wasn't much to do while he waited. Bending down, Danny pried at the thing. After a few seconds struggling, he managed to wrestle it out of the mud. He held it up in what little light there was.

It was a box of some sort—about a foot long, six inches wide, and the same deep. Danny stared at it in wonder. What could it be? Maybe the treasure from the house that the two killers had been looking for?

"Danny!"

He jerked back to reality as Tracy's dad called his name. "You can climb up now!"

"Coming," Danny called. Holding the box awkwardly under one arm, Danny began slowly climbing up the ladder.

Finally, his head emerged into daylight. Then he was off the wood. Then Danny collapsed into a heap on the ground. He felt completely drained. All he wanted to do was to rest.

Nicole looked at him in worry. "You okay?"

"I guess." Danny realized he was still clutching the box under his arm.

"Come on," Mr. McCall said firmly. "Your aunt took Tracy home. Now you're all getting out of here and I'm

going to have the fence boarded up properly. You kids
should have known better than to play here.''

With that, Danny could only agree. But . . . would Zack
let them stay away? Or would that mysterious force pull
Danny back again?

Chapter Eleven

TWO AGAINST ONE

Back at the house, Danny slipped the box into a plastic bag and put it in his tent. Then he showered and changed out of his muddy clothes. Heading back to his tent with a screwdriver to force open the box, he ran into Nicole. She had put on a sweater, despite the fact that it was summer, and Danny could understand why. The touch of the ghost left a chill right through to the bone.

"We'd better talk," she told him, grimly. "I want to know what's going on."

Danny glanced back at the house. Brandon was inside, playing one of his video games. Kate was off with her Barbie dolls. There was no sign of Aunt Sandy. "Okay," he said. He told Nicole what had happened to him. She listened straight through without interrupting him at all. Then she stared at him, thoughtfully.

"If I hadn't felt that cold spot and seen the ghost, too, I'd think you were psycho," she told him. "But I don't understand what's going on."

"I don't either," he admitted. "It's like Zackary is playing a sick game of tag with living things. If he touches them, they freeze. If he *squeezes* them, they die and he gets more real. At least for a little while."

"He didn't kill either of us," Nicole pointed out.

"I think he tried to," Danny told her. "But Brandon interrupted him by accident. And I knocked you away from him deliberately." He snapped his fingers. "And it was only *after* he touched us that we actually started to see him," he said excitedly. "I could see him attacking you, but you didn't see a thing."

"Right," agreed Nicole, slowly. "And now we can both see him." She shuddered and looked over her shoulder. "I think I'd rather *not* know when I'm being haunted!" Then she frowned. "But what's he after?"

Danny shrugged. "He's got some sort of creepy plan, I think. I can sometimes kind of slip into his mind, and see things he can see. It seems like he's up to something. I just can't make out what it is." He looked at her and smiled weakly. "Actually, I'm kind of glad you saw Zack, too. It means I'm not going nuts."

"Yeah." She glanced toward the boys' tent. "What about that box you found? Does it have something to do with Zack?"

"I don't know," he replied. "I found it in the pit where Tracy was."

"Maybe it's some buried treasure," Nicole suggested excitedly.

Danny shook his head. "I thought that at first. But it's kind of small for anything valuable."

83

"It could be jewelry," answered Nicole. "That doesn't take up much room. And it's worth lots of money. Come on, let's look at it!"

They went to the tent, and Danny pulled the filthy box out of the bag. He knocked off as much mud as he could, then used the screwdriver point to scrape the grooves around the lid clean. There was no sign of a lock, but the box was tightly shut.

Maybe it really did contain something valuable. With increasing excitement, Danny pried at it with the screwdriver. Finally, the lid popped open and they stared inside.

It wasn't treasure, after all. In the box lay an old wooden spinning top and a small whip.

Danny looked at them closely. "Wait a minute; I've seen these before. At the Historical Society there's a painting of Zack and his parents. Zack's holding these toys in his hand."

"I'd like to burn them," Nicole said angrily. "I'd like to burn *him*."

Danny fingered the top thoughtfully. It might be an idea, just to show Zack what they thought of him. Then, underneath the top, he saw something else. "Hey!" He pulled at it and a small wad of paper came out in his hands. He unfolded it.

It was writing paper of some sort, yellow and crinkly. The edges were eaten away, and the writing on the paper was badly faded.

Nicole was peering over his shoulder. "I can't read it," she complained.

"I can't either," Danny admitted. "But maybe this is some sort of a clue," he suggested. "If it's in Zack's toy box, it must have been important to him."

"What difference does it make?" Nicole sighed. "We can't read it."

Danny grinned. "Maybe the lady at the Historical Society can!" he said. "They're used to dealing with moldy old things there."

"Would she bother?" asked Nicole.

Danny tapped the box. "I'll bet she'd love to have these toys to go with that painting they have on display," he said. "She's bound to want to read the letter, too."

Nicole shrugged doubtfully. "It's worth a try," she agreed. "You want to bike down or see if Mom'll give us a ride?"

Aunt Sandy was in the kitchen, the keys to the van jangling in her hand. She looked up as they came in. "I'm off to the drugstore. Between Danny's knee and this morning's adventure I'm out of antiseptic. And at the rate you kids are going, I better stay prepared."

"Can we come, too?" asked Nicole. "Danny found a box down the pit. It's got some old toys in it. We thought they might like them at the Historical Society."

"Sure," Aunt Sandy said, a little surprised.

It was a short trip into town, and Aunt Sandy dropped them outside the brick building. "Stay there, and I'll pick you up on my way back," she said.

Danny led the way in as she drove off. The same woman he'd met the other day was there. She looked up from her reading a little surprised to see him. "Well," she

85

said. "This is a pleasure. Did you find our little museum so entertaining last time?" Before he could reply, the lady peered down at Nicole. "And who's this? Your girl-friend?"

Danny and Nicole just looked at each other. "She's my cousin," Danny told her. "We're staying with her family while my folks hunt for a house."

"Actually," Nicole said quickly, "we brought you something you might want for your museum." Danny showed her the box, and then opened it up.

"Goodness!" she exclaimed. "How interesting. An old-fashioned top and whip." Then she did a double take. "Wherever did you get this?"

"On the grounds of the old Powell house," Danny told her. "It's the same one that Zackary is holding in the painting you've got upstairs."

The woman nodded. "Yes," she agreed. "I do believe you're right. Let's check, shall we?" She led the way to the stairs. "This would be the second authentic relic of the Powells that we've found," she went on. She pointed to one of the model boats. "That's a scale model of the Captain's boat." Then she marched them up the stairs and down the hallway to the painting.

Danny waited for Nicole's reaction. For a moment, she looked blankly at it; then, her eyes were drawn to those of Zack in the painting.

"It's just like him," she whispered.

"Like someone you know?" asked the woman.

"Right!" said Danny and Nicole in the same instant.

The woman compared the top and whip in the picture

to the ones in the box. "You know, you're absolutely right. These are the same toys. Most interesting!"

Danny removed the whip and showed her the letter. "This was in the box, too," he explained. "But it's all faded and old. Is there any way that you could help us read it?"

The old lady took the papers and opened them carefully. "I see what you mean," she said. Danny had a sinking feeling that it was hopeless. Then she glanced up and winked at him. "Luckily I know a few tricks we can try," she said.

She went to one of the cupboards under the old photos and pulled out what looked like a small table with an electrical cord. Seeing their puzzled expressions, she smiled. "This is a light box," she explained, plugging it in. "It's for looking at slides." Flicking on a switch made the top light up. "Normally we use it to select slides for the monthly lectures, but it should do the trick for this old letter, too. Taking the first page of the letter, she placed it carefully down on the lighted panel and adjusted her glasses. "Much better!" she said happily. The light coming through the paper really made the writing show up. "I think I can make it out now. It's addressed *My Dearest Elizabeth. . . .*" She broke off. "My, this is exciting! It must have been written by Captain Powell to his wife! This really is a find!"

"Will you please read it to us?" Nicole asked.

Chapter Twelve

THE CAPTAIN'S TALE

"My Dearest Elizabeth," she read.

"I'm writing this letter to you during a short stopover in Spain. You always express so much interest in my trips, and they are so often nothing more than dull, day-to-day routine. But my latest trip has proven to be anything but normal. While I wait for my ship to be loaded again, I thought I would tell my strange story to you.

"A month or so ago, we were sailing around the Cape of Good Hope in the most dreadful weather. The Cape is a difficult passage at the best of times. The weather there is changeable, and the seas difficult to navigate. This time, the waves were huge, almost swamping the ship, and thunder and lightning raged all about us. Then came one bolt of lightning larger than any I've witnessed in all my years at sea. It struck the

main mast and set the sails and rigging alight, even in all of the crashing rain.

"It was a tense few minutes, I can tell you now. At that moment, I was not sure whether we would live or die. The men had to cut the rigging free. It was swept overboard into the tremendous waves and lost in seconds. Then the mast split in two—the force of the lightning must have shattered the wood. The top half fell over the side of the ship, taking with it two deckhands. Both men and mast vanished instantly into the raging waves and were never seen again. At any second, we all expected to join them.

"Then, as suddenly as it had begun to rage, the wind died down almost to a calm. Fifteen minutes later, you would not have known that there had been a storm if it weren't for the damage to my poor ship.

"Without the main mast, we could only limp along. We had to replace it, else we would never make a safe port again. But we were miles from the nearest land—at least, according to my best charts. Then there was a cry from the lookout that there was land on the port bow.

"Land meant trees, and there might be a chance to repair our broken ship. It took our damaged boat a long time, but eventually we gained the small, isolated island.

"We found a goodly bay, sheltered from the winds and high seas, and cast anchor as close to the shore as we dared. I assembled a small landing party and lowered the longboat. As we rowed closer, we could see that the island was densely wooded.

"We pulled ashore and began our survey. I began to despair, for all the trees we came upon were stunted and gnarled. Then, toward the center of the island, we found it. In a small clearing stood a tree. It was perfect, the only one of its kind on the island. Tall and straight and wonderfully hard, it would be our salvation.

"I ordered my men to fell the tree but, before ax hit wood, we were interrupted. A strange figure appeared from the surrounding woods. A tall man of proud bearing, he wore an extraordinary cloak made of an entire lion skin. The forelegs were tied around his neck, and the skull settled over his head.

"He knew few words of English—learned who knew how? But he knew enough to make clear his meaning. He claimed the tree held a powerful spirit and could not be cut down.

"The lives of my men depended on me. We needed that tree or we would all be doomed. I thought, too, of you and sweet Zackary waiting for me.

"I tried to reason with the man, to no avail. As he saw that we meant to go ahead, he became frenzied and wild. He lunged at me and, I'm sorry to say, was shot by my crew who thought he meant to harm me.

"As my men prepared to cut the tree, I did what I could to ease the suffering of the wounded man. I'm afraid his injury was too grievous. He lay dying, cursing me for freeing the evil spirit imprisoned in the tree.

"As he gasped his dying breath, I heard the crashing of the great tree as it was brought to the ground. With a terrible cry, the lion-man died in my arms. Before we left the small island with our precious cargo for the replacement mast, I had my men bury him. Strange and maddened figure though he was, he was still a man for all that. I was sorry we could not save him.

"Once we'd repaired the ship—a matter of a day, no more—we sailed for Spain.

"This has been the strangest journey. I can't wait to see you and my beloved boy again. I am sending this letter to you by the hand of another captain whose ship departs this morning for Boston. If we should run into further delays, at least you will have this letter to keep me in your hearts until my return.

With sincere affection,
Your loving husband, Elijah."

The Historical Society lady looked up from the letter and sighed. "It's dated shortly before he vanished forever," she told Danny and Nicole. "His ship must have sunk on the voyage home. How sad." Then she brightened up. "But we at least have this letter to add to our collection! How wonderful! Our president, Mr. Tupper, will want to hear about this find immediately. Oh, I'm so thrilled!" She beamed at the two of them, and then almost ran back downstairs.

Danny barely paid attention. He was thinking about the eerie story he'd just heard.

Nicole stared at the painting again. "Spooky, isn't it?"

"And it's going to get a whole lot spookier," said a voice they both remembered well. It sounded like it was coming from *inside* the painting. It sounded like the sighing of the wind in the trees. . . .

They both watched in horror as the picture of Zackary seemed to shiver, and then the ghost walked straight out of the painting at them. He was grinning crazily.

Chapter Thirteen

THE COMPANY OF SPIRITS

Nicole and Danny clutched each other for comfort and backed slowly away from Zack. Zackary looked very pleased with himself. "You thought I was stuck just at the old house, didn't you?" he asked. "Well, I was. But I'm not anymore."

"The toys!" Nicole said, suddenly realizing.

"That's right," Zackary agreed, casually. He looked back at the painting. It made Danny giddy, looking at the painted Zackary through the ghost of the real one. "Isn't that a terrible picture?" he asked them. "I never did like it. Makes me look so . . . oh, so sweet and innocent, I guess."

A shiver ran up Danny's spine. "What are you talking about?"

"Doesn't it make you want to throw up?" asked Zackary. "I mean—the classic happy family picture. As if it was like that!"

93

Nicole gave Danny a look. "You weren't happy, then?" she said carefully.

"Happy?" Zack snorted. "I wasn't happy alive, and let me tell you that being dead isn't exactly a bundle of joy, either. Watching kids like you play and have fun, and do things—and not being able to be a part of it." He sounded more angry than sad. He pointed to the captain. "There we are—Captain Elijah Powell, the great trader, and wealthiest man in the area. And he just left me and my mother and went off and never came back. And whatever happened to all of that money—money that should have been *mine* when I grew up? Nothing! Mama kept saying she'd spent it all. But I knew better. She wanted to keep it for herself. She was going to starve me to death, so she wouldn't have to share any of it with me. But I fixed her."

Danny suddenly understood. He pointed a shaking finger at the ghost. "It was you! *You* were the one who told Wright and Gower that there was treasure in the house, weren't you?"

"That's right." Zack's eyes burned angrily now. "I let them in on the secret and offered them a share if they helped me get what belonged to me."

Nicole gave him a filthy look. "You're disgusting!" she said. "You let them kill your own mother!"

"She was trying to cheat me," Zack replied, not at all bothered by their feelings. "She deserved it. But she wouldn't tell us where the money and gold were hidden. So Gower killed her. Then we tore the house apart looking for the gold."

"And when there wasn't any," Danny guessed, "they

killed you, too, thinking it was a trick you'd played on them.'' He glared furiously at the ghost. ''And to think I once felt sorry for you! You're worse than dog vomit. You *deserved* to be murdered.''

''I don't care what you think,'' Zack said, sneering. ''You've still helped me do what I wanted. Bringing those toys here helped my plans a whole lot.''

Danny frowned. ''I don't get it.''

''Boy, you modern kids really are stupid, aren't you?'' Zack shrugged. ''Ghosts are sort of tied to things that belonged to them, I guess. I was stuck with the old house, because that's where all of my life had been spent. If I moved too far from it, I had to go back. It's like a long piece of elastic, pulling me in. But those toys and that model ship and this picture were part of my life, too. Now that they're here, it's like I've got some extra stretch. I can choose to come here now, if I want to.''

''Big deal,'' Danny said. ''So you're in a prison with two rooms instead of just one. What difference does it make?''

''What would you know about the difference it makes?'' Zackary sneered. ''What do you know about anything?''

He glared at Danny and Nicole with such hatred in his eyes it was almost physical. Danny and Nicole cringed away from him.

''Afraid of me, huh? You don't know the meaning of terror . . . yet!'' Zackary taunted them.

''Yoo-hoo!'' It was the old lady, hollering up to them

from downstairs. Hearing her call out so ridiculously just made everything seem that much more ghoulish.

"I say, I'm closing up now!" she called again.

As Zack continued to stare malevolently at Danny and Nicole, they turned and fled.

THE FINAL DREAM

Danny was dreaming. Once again, he was inside Zackary Powell. He could feel what Zackary felt. He could hear Zackary's thoughts. This time, though, he wasn't alone with Zack. Nicole was there, too.

"Danny?" Her voice sounded thin and wavery. "What's going on?"

"This is what I told you about," he explained. "The dreams where I follow along with Zack."

"But he doesn't seem to hear you like I can."

"I know." Danny answered. "I don't think he knows about this part of things. I'm sure he doesn't control it. Let's see what he's doing."

Danny realized this was another time when he was watching something that happened to Zack in the past.

A family was living in the old house.

"A family named Graebel used to live there," came Nicole's whisper. "They moved away when I was really little."

Zack went right through the closed front door. He carefully climbed the stairs, then paused. Turning to the right, he walked down to the end of the hall and into a doorway.

It was a nursery. Inside was a small crib, and over it hung a mobile. Danny vaguely remembered that his sister had once had a room like that. Zack crossed to the crib and looked down.

There was a baby in there, fast asleep. Zack tensed, and Danny suddenly knew what the ghost was up to.

"No!" he screamed, and tried to do something. But he couldn't. Zack still seemed to be completely unaware of him. Nicole understood what was happening, too, and tried to fight it. But she had as little effect as Danny did.

Reaching into the crib, Zack slid his hand into the baby's chest. Then, a twisted grin on his face, he clenched his fist and squeezed.

The baby gave a sudden cry, and went rigid under the evil hand of Zack Powell. Danny and Nicole both raged and screamed, but Zack didn't pay the slightest attention.

He was killing the baby, and they couldn't stop him!

There was an explosive tingle inside of Zack now. This was stronger and more powerful than he'd ever felt. His arm became solid again, and the world started to take shape about him. The darkness of night settled in. They could hear the gasping of the tiny infant.

Suddenly, a shape loomed in the doorway. It was a woman—"Mrs. Graebel!" Nicole breathed. Mrs. Graebel screamed. Then, rushing forward, she yelled, "Get away from my baby!" She swung her fist in Zack's face.

To everyone's surprise—especially Zack's—the fist

smacked his nose hard. Stunned, he was knocked clear of the crib. Mrs. Graebel snatched up the child, hugging it to her. It started hiccuping, almost blue with the cold from Zack's fist.

Zack, in pain such as he hadn't felt in ages, lay on the floor, whimpering.

Then the world started to turn back to that ghostly light again. Zack began to fade. Mrs. Graebel reeled away, staring at him in horror. Then Zack simply faded out completely, and she knew that she'd been seeing a ghost.

"So that's why they moved away," Nicole told Danny. "They thought their house was haunted!"

"And they were afraid Zack would come back and kill their baby," Danny added.

As Zack had grown more ghostlike and less solid, his pain had faded. But he was badly shaken. He fled. He didn't stop running through everything until the terrible tugging held him clinging to a broken-down corner of the fence. There he seemed to shrink inside of himself and was almost weeping.

"I nearly had it!" he sobbed. "I nearly had it. I could feel it. If only I'd killed that ugly little useless thing, I'd be real again. I know it! But she stopped me."

With a dreadful, sickening feeling, it all made sense to Danny now. He knew what Zack was up to.

The smaller forms of life—the insects and birds, that sort of thing—had given Zack some kind of life-spark. But it didn't last, because it was tiny and meant for some small creature. It faded away fast when Zack took it. The cat had been better, because it had been larger and had more of the life-force in it. Zack had felt alive for quite a while after that killing.

The baby had been the closest of them all. It had a human-sized life-force. Zack wanted to steal the baby's life-force, to become alive again.

That was why he had tried to tag Danny. When that hadn't worked, he'd gone after Nicole. He had taken *some* energy from them, but he hadn't been able to drain them completely. It had made him real enough to see. But not real enough to last.

"That's why we're here now," Nicole spoke into Danny's thoughts. "He's got part of *us*—our life-forces— inside him now. Just a little, and very spread out. In the daytime we don't even notice it's missing. But when we're asleep, we link up with him through it."

Danny had to admit that it made a sort of crazy sense.

Zack was aiming to kill someone, to take *all* of his life-energy and to become alive again. Either Danny or Nicole if he could. Danny felt sick.

Still, it took time for Zack to kill somebody. It was a hard job, and he needed peace. Any interruptions would break the bond. That had saved the baby, and it had saved them.

But now . . . those toys were in the Historical Society. Zack could go there at any time! And that poor lady who sat all day at the entrance, reading her silly romances . . . she would be all alone. She wouldn't even know Zack was there.

ZACK ATTACK

The dream was not quite over. Even as the sickening truth about Zack's plans came to Danny, he was forced to watch. The scene had shifted now to the Historical Society, and Danny realized that he had now reached the present. What he and Nicole were now witnessing was either happening right this moment, or could have happened only a few hours ago.

Zack was prowling about the building like a caged tiger. A rage was growing inside him by the minute. He stomped by the model ships, past the Indian arrowheads, and right through the collections of old photographs.

"No one!" he howled angrily. "There's nobody here! All of this . . . junk from the past, and no other ghosts. Where? Where are they?"

Where were they? Danny found his own thoughts getting confused with Zack's. Okay, *Zack* was a ghost—why was he still hanging around his old home? Why hadn't he gone where the others now were?

"Maybe it's because he won't let go," Nicole said. "When he died, he was still after the treasure he thought was in his house. So he stayed there. Maybe he had a chance to go on, but didn't. And now he's still hanging on, trying to bring himself back to life. He won't *let* himself leave. Maybe that's why he's all alone."

"I'm not giving up," they heard Zack mutter. "I'm going to win. I'm going to make it. Tomorrow morning, when that silly old hag comes in here . . ." He clenched his fist and smiled to himself. "After all, *I* can put all that energy to better use than she can. I deserve it, and she doesn't."

Then he looked about the room again, seeing all of the ancient relics that meant nothing to him. "It isn't fair!" he screamed out. "But it will be. . . ."

At that moment, Danny woke up with a gasp. His eyes came into focus, and he saw that it was morning. A ray of sunlight had fallen across his face. He rolled over and saw that Brandon was still fast asleep. He slid out of his bag and then out of the tent. The grass under his bare feet was still wet.

Nicole, in her pajamas, was also outside. She gave Danny a look of total despair. "It's today," she said. "Zack's going to kill that poor old lady today, and then become real again."

"I know," said Danny, grimly. "And I'll tell you something else. I'll bet the first thing he'll do afterward is come for us. We're the only ones who know his secrets, and he knows we can give him away."

Nicole looked scared. "What can we do?"

"We have to stop him somehow," Danny told her. "Before he kills that lady and becomes alive again."

"How?" asked Nicole.

"I don't know," Danny admitted. "Let's get dressed fast and think about it."

The clock showed it was just before eight. They could hear someone in the upstairs bathroom. When they were both washed and dressed, they went into the kitchen. Aunt Sandy was making a pot of coffee.

"Couldn't sleep?" she asked.

Nicole nodded as Aunt Sandy handed them both glasses of orange juice.

"Um, Aunt Sandy?" Danny asked as he got out cereal and milk for him and Nicole.

"Mmm-hmm," she answered absently, trying to slip her mug under the coffee drip so she wouldn't have to wait for the whole pot to brew through.

"Can me and Nicole take our bikes out?" Danny blurted.

"Nicole and I," Aunt Sandy corrected. "Sure, why not? You're not going too far, I hope."

"Oh, no," Nicole assured her, catching on to Danny's idea. "We're just going to take a spin around town after breakfast."

"Fine, fine. You two have fun," Aunt Sandy said, taking her coffee mug into the den with the newspaper. "Me, I'm going to enjoy this wonderfully quiet morning my own way."

Danny and Nicole ate their cereal quickly. It was a little after eight o'clock by the time they were finished. Danny figured it would take about an hour to pedal into town, and he remembered that the sign outside the Historical Society listed its hours as 9:30 A.M. to 4:00 P.M.

With luck, they'd get there in plenty of time.

It seemed to take forever for them to get to the center of town. There was a lot of traffic, and they had to go carefully. Danny's watch seemed to be rushing toward nine thirty. What if they weren't in time to save the Historical Society lady?

Finally, out of breath and with aching legs, Danny skidded to a halt in front of the brick building. Leaving their bikes on the ground, they dashed up to the door. Danny reached it first and turned the handle. It was unlocked!

Throwing the door open, they charged inside, fearing the worst.

The woman was standing just inside. She looked up in surprise, then smiled when she recognized them. "You two must *really* be keen on history," she said. "You didn't even give me time to open up or take off my coat." The door to the main part of the building was still closed.

"You can't stay here!" Danny told her. "It isn't safe."

"You *mustn't* stay," added Nicole. "He'll kill you if you do!"

The lady laughed. "Why ever do *you* want to kill *me?*" she asked Danny.

"Not *me,*" Danny snapped. "The ghost of Zackary Powell."

"Oh, that old story." Unworried, the lady put her coat across the back of her chair and took a key from her bag.

"Believe me, young man, at my age, I'm not afraid of ghosts."

"Perhaps you should be," Nicole said.

"Well, maybe so," the woman agreed, a twinkle in her eye. "It's a game of some sort, right? Never let it be said that Mrs. Irene Gower didn't know how to play."

"Mrs. *Gower?*" asked Danny, his blood running cold. "You're not related to the Gower who was a murderer two hundred years ago, are you?"

Mrs. Gower smiled, resignedly. "The black sheep in the family closet," she admitted. "Not mine. My husband's. That Gower you speak of was his many times great-grand-uncle. And a nasty man, too, by all accounts."

"And he was one of the men who killed Zack," breathed Nicole. She looked at Danny. "Do you think he knows who she is?"

"Who cares?" snapped Danny. "He wants to kill her anyway."

"What *are* you talking about?" Mrs. Gower asked. "What kind of game is this?"

Rather than answering, Nicole asked, "That box of toys we brought you yesterday, what did you do with it?"

"I put it upstairs on a small table under the painting of the Powell family." Mrs. Gower gave them a grateful smile. "I thought it looked very good there. I can't thank you enough for donating it. We're having a card made up, you know. And we'll put both of your names on it if you like."

"No, you won't," Danny said, grimly.

Mrs. Gower paused as she unlocked the inner door,

puzzled. "What on earth are you going on about?" she asked. "You're making me quite dizzy. What kind of game is this?"

Danny shot her a look. "It's a deadly game of tag," he said seriously. Mrs. Gower had finished unlocking the main door. Danny grabbed her arm. "Maybe Nicole and I should go first," he said. "We've got to get to those toys first," he added, more to himself than Mrs. Gower. Carefully, he pushed the door slowly open.

Everything seemed to be perfectly normal. The exhibits were neat and tidy, and there wasn't a sound. Nicole nudged him, and they walked quietly into the main room. Danny began to wonder if they *were* wrong. Nothing looked out of place. There was no sign at all of Zack. Had it all been some weird sort of nightmare?

"Haven't you two had enough yet?"

Danny jumped, and so did Nicole. Zack stood at the top of the stairs, glaring down at them. They could see the paintings on the wall behind him through his body. Danny swallowed hard. "Get out," he said boldly.

Zack threw his head back and laughed. "Or what?" he jeered. "There's nothing you can do to me. But plenty I can do to you."

"Who are you talking to?" asked Mrs. Gower, a slight frown on her face.

"Zack Powell," Danny told her. "He's at the top of the stairs."

"Really?" Mrs. Gower came into the room. "This is most exciting. Do you mean to tell me that you think this place is haunted by a real ghost?"

"We don't *think* it; we know it," Nicole told her, fingering the matchbook in her pocket. Their plan was for Danny to distract Zack while Nicole destroyed the old toys by burning them.

The old lady shook her head. "Well, you wanted to get to those toys right away, right?"

"The toys?" Zack glanced over his shoulder, and then back down at them. His face clouded with fury as he realized what they were planning. "So that's what you're up to! You're trying to get rid of me! Well, it won't work!"

"Nice going," Danny muttered, glaring at Mrs. Gower.

"Oh, dear." She looked very sorry. "Have I spoiled the game?"

"This isn't a game!" Danny yelled. "It's all real. We keep trying to tell you."

Zack slowly moved down the stairs toward them, watching carefully. "You're not going to touch my toys," he vowed. "I'll kill you if you even try."

"You've tried to kill us before, and it didn't work," Danny sneered. "You're a total klutz, a useless loser, you know that?"

"Why, you . . ." Zack snarled, and then started moving faster, intent on getting his tormenter. "You'll never tease me again. I'll see to that!"

"Break right!" Danny hissed to Nicole. He didn't wait to see if she obeyed him, but dived to the left. He dodged past the showcases and ran toward the large windows. He was close to the model ships here. Looking back at the stairs, he saw Nicole shooting off among the bookcases.

Zack stood there, looking from one of them to the other. He didn't seem able to decide whom to go after first.

Danny grimly hoped that Zack hadn't figured out what he was up to. He stood up and jeered at the ghost. "You're such a failure, Zack!" he yelled. "You can't get me!"

Enraged, Zack rushed after Danny. Mrs. Gower stood bewildered by the door, watching Danny and Nicole race around and talk with someone she couldn't see. She probably thought they were both crazy, Danny guessed, but at least she was safe for now. If only he could say the same about himself!

While he kept Zack mad and distracted, maybe Nicole could get to work. All Danny had to do was to dodge Zack until then. . . . He waited till Zack was almost on him, then ducked under the table holding the model of the prerevolutionary town. On hands and knees, he scuttled along, then jumped to his feet.

Zack was right in front of him, waiting. He grinned nastily. "I don't have to go around or under things," he said. He raised his arm, his hand reaching for Danny. Danny started to back away. His legs collided with a display case. There wasn't anywhere to go.

Just as it looked like Zack was going to tag him, Mrs. Gower called out: "My dear, please be careful. And what is that in your hand?"

Zack glanced around and stiffened in shock. He could see Nicole stumbling up the stairs. She held the matchbook in her hand and was trying to light one as she ran.

"No!" he screamed, half in anger, half in fear. He turned to go after her.

Heedless of his own safety, Danny jumped at Zack to try and stop him. His hands passed right through the ghost, who was already off and running incredibly fast. Danny stumbled clear through the misty figure, and into a display case. A sharp pain lanced through his shoulder where he struck the heavy wooden frame.

Nicole saw that Zack was after her. Danny could see she was almost at the top of the stairs, but the painting and toys were a long way off yet. She'd never make it in time.

Zack had one more trick up his sleeve. With a tremendous leap, he seemed to sail through the air, and down onto Nicole. As Zack landed on her back like a cat, he thrust his hand into her, and then *squeezed* with his fist.

Nicole gave a terrible cry, and went rigid. She crashed down at the top step, her numb fingers letting go of the matchbook. It fell down the stairs toward Danny. His face twisted in fury, Zack concentrated on his task.

Chapter Sixteen

DEAD RECKONING

"No!" screamed Danny in horror. "Let her go!"

Bewildered, Mrs. Gower stared. "What's happening?" she asked. "Is she having a fit?"

Zack looked down the stairs at them, triumph on his face. "You can't stop me," he gloated. "In just a few seconds, I'll have her life-force. I'll be real again, and she'll be dead."

"Don't do it," Danny begged. "Zack, *please*, let her go."

"Not a chance," Zack answered. "Not now that I'm so close. There's nothing you can do." He turned his back on Danny, and concentrated.

Danny tried to ignore the pain in his shoulder, and he staggered away from the display case. He was right next to the model ships now, and he stumbled again, crashing into the table. The model of Captain Powell's ship was jarred from its supports. With a yell of wordless rage,

Danny snatched it up and threw it as hard as he could at the floor.

The model didn't even reach the floor. Instead, it seemed to float in the air, as if on some invisible ocean. It moved gently toward the stairs. Danny followed after it, stunned. Was this some new trick of Zack's?

The room seemed to be changing. Danny saw deep fear in Mrs. Gower's eyes. She had finally accepted that something supernatural was really happening. There seemed to be a brackish smell, and an awful damp pervaded the air. Wind started to pluck at their hair and clothes.

''What on earth? . . .'' Mrs. Gower stammered.

Finally, even Zack seemed to notice that something weird was going on. He glanced around, and then stiffened in shock when he saw the ship, floating in the air, rising toward him. With a jerk, he jumped to his feet, freeing Nicole.

With a deep, loud intake of breath, she fell to her knees on the landing. She was shivering and looked scared and drawn. But at least she was still alive. Slowly, she looked up toward Zack and her eyes widened.

The ghost was backing away from the rising ship. The wind was rattling the cases around the room and shaking the pictures on the wall. The smell of the sea and moist breezes were growing stronger, and the room seemed to be swaying. It was as if the room was somehow afloat and miles out at sea.

Nicole stumbled down the stairs and clutched Danny tightly. He didn't care that she felt like a block of ice. He needed to hold onto someone right then, too.

A jagged flash of lightning snapped across the room, followed by a hollow boom of thunder. Mrs. Gower screamed.

There was a crash, and suddenly the room seemed filled with noise. Danny could hear the creaking sounds of a wooden ship at sea. The planks were complaining, moaning in time with each roll of a wave. Crash! And another huge wave broke, sending the creaking ship forward once more.

Overhead, there was the snapping sound of a sail catching a strong wind, straining to break free. Ropes held it in place, and it howled out its misery. Crash! And the ship pitched forward once more. It seemed huge now. It wasn't a model anymore, but a real ship, sailing some ghostly ocean that thundered and roared about the three small humans and one terrified ghost-boy.

Lightning zagged across the ceiling again, and a sheet of rain fell, drenching everything. Danny shivered, his clothes soaked and sticking to his skin. The wind screamed like some mad demon, and the lightning strobed again.

This time, there were more people there. The ship seemed to be filled with them. It was hard in the growing gloom to make out many details, and the ones that Danny could make out, he wished he hadn't. They seemed to have all kinds of shapes and sizes and were muttering to themselves and to others. The voices ran together, making sounds that rose and fell like the waves. They didn't sound human—more like fingernails on chalkboards. Danny shivered as the sounds grated on his nerves.

The ship seemed to have stopped moving and now just floated along on the ghostly waves. Though the rain was soaking Danny and the others, the ocean didn't seem to be quite as real. If it had been, they would all have drowned.

How the ship managed to grow was weird enough, but as it floated there, Danny could see that its masts must have passed beyond the roof and that some of the hull must be outside.

Danny and Nicole weren't the only ones who were shaking with fear. Danny glanced back, and saw that Mrs. Gower was just as wet and white. Even as he looked, the old lady took a sighing breath, and fainted dead away.

But if the living people were scared, it was nothing compared to what Zack was going through. He looked as if he'd shrunk, and he was trembling like a leaf in high wind. He couldn't drag his eyes away from the ship.

Zack was staring as if hypnotized at the ship's main mast. Danny followed his gaze, and stiffened in shock. There was a man chained to it. Thick, clanking chains bound his ankles and arms. The man's clothes were barely more than rags clinging to his body. He was white-haired and bearded, and his face was twisted in agony. But the most horrible thing of all was that Danny recognized that face.

It was battered, and strained, and streaked with blood. But it was quite clearly the same face that gazed from the oil painting down the corridor. The man chained to the mast of this ghastly, ghostly ship was Captain Powell.

Zack's long-dead father.

Chapter Seventeen

VOYAGE TO ETERNITY

Danny looked across at Nicole. She was almost as pale as the ghosts herself. She, too, had recognized the man fastened to the mast.

There was a sudden movement on the ship, and in the next bright flash of lightning, Danny saw that there was a strangely dressed figure at the ship's rail. He heard Nicole's squeal of terror, but there was nothing really scary about the man.

He was tall, thin, and straight, and his skin glittered wetly in each flash of lightning. He was dressed in an astonishing lion-skin cloak. The lion's top jaw rested on the man's head. The teeth were still in it, and they looked almost like little curls of hair across his forehead.

This strange figure looked at Zack, and laughed. It was not a nice laugh. It didn't sound like there was any humor in it. Just a lot of pain, and also some triumph. "So," he called out, his voice deep and echoing. "So, Zackary Powell, it has come to this, has it?"

Zack seemed to be trying to slip into the wall of the picture gallery, to escape from this ghostly greeting. But it wasn't working. He was stuck.

The lion-clad figure continued to look at Zack for a moment; then, he shook his head. "We've been more than patient with you. But you mistook our patience for weakness, Zackary Powell. You've learned nothing at all from your punishment. Instead, you've tried to escape it by trading places with the living."

For the first time, he seemed to notice the three human beings. He gave a low bow in their direction. "My apologies for what you have suffered," he told them. "It was not supposed to have happened, but"—he shot a grim look at Zack—"I tend to be a little too lenient where children are concerned." Then he laughed. "Though since he's two hundred years old, he could hardly be called a child, could he?"

Danny didn't know what to say. He wasn't exactly afraid of the ghostly man—somehow he wasn't scary, like Zack. But he was very, very strange. Like he belonged somewhere else and not here. He was just passing by, and for a moment their worlds were linked together. Danny looked into the man's eyes, and it seemed like there were a billion stars inside, and they went on forever. He had a giddy feeling, like he could be falling into those dark eyes. Then Danny snapped his head away, and the man laughed.

"You'll do fine, boy." He looked at Nicole and winked. "You too, girl." He nodded, as if satisfied about something unspoken.

"It's the witch doctor!" Nicole said. "The one who cursed Captain Powell when he cut down the spirit tree." Danny nodded dumbly.

The lion-man turned back to Zack, who was trying to crawl away on his hands and knees. His eyes shone with a fierce rage. "You can't escape like that," he said softly. "There was only one way to escape the chains that have been made for you, and you wouldn't take it. So you'll have to take them instead."

The man made an overhand throwing motion, like he was tossing a baseball. Danny couldn't see anything, but Zack screamed and tried to dodge away. There was a second of intense light, and then Zack gave a single, terrible scream.

When Danny's eyes cleared, Zack was no longer in the painting gallery. He was on the ship, chained to the largest mast, just as his father had been. He seemed to be screaming, because his mouth was open. But no sound from him reached them over the raging storm. The lion-man looked at Captain Powell, who now stood shaking on the water-soaked deck. His chains had slipped away, and he was staring down at his hands as if he couldn't believe he was free.

"It's over," the witch doctor said. "You've paid for your crimes. As I told you two hundred years ago, when the wood is broken, the spirit is freed—but someone must take his place." He glared across at Zackary. "And he has been found."

With a great cry, half-pain and half-hope, the old captain reached out toward his son. But he never managed to touch the chained ghost. Instead, his figure faded away to nothing as the wind and rain howled around the now-empty space.

The lion-man looked down at Danny and Nicole. "It is time for us to go. Zackary Powell has taken his father's place, and my voyage must go on."

"What . . . what's gonna happen to him?" asked Danny. He was astonished to find he could even speak.

The man shook his head. "That you do not want to know. But he will never bother you again."

"The toys," Nicole said, "what about them?"

"They're just . . . toys," the figure told her. "His link has been shattered. They cannot harm anyone now." He turned away, and then, as if in afterthought, turned back. "But he took something from each of you." He strode across the deck, ignoring the wind, rain, and waves as if they didn't exist. Danny supposed that they didn't, really, but the lion-man was the only person who seemed unaffected by them.

Stopping beside Zack, the man reached out his own hand, and then twisted it in the air. He walked back to the side of the ship, and made another throwing gesture. Something bright sparkled in the air and then split into two parts. One of these shot toward Danny and buried itself in his chest. The other went to Nicole.

Immediately, Danny felt stronger. The storm seemed a little less intense, his clothes a little less wet. The noises faded. The man laughed down at them. "The life-energy he stole from you, it's back where it belongs. You'll share no more of his dreams and nightmares."

117

Then he waved. "Goodbye. And pray you never need to see me again."

He turned away a final time. The lightning flashed again, and the thunder rolled. But it seemed to be losing its strength. The ship creaked and groaned and then started moving. It dipped away from them into the phantom sea. A huge wave made the ship rear a little, and they caught one last glimpse of Zack, chained to his mast, and then the ship slowly faded away.

Chapter Eighteen

HOME

Still soaked through, Danny climbed to his feet. Nicole rose beside him to survey the museum.

It looked like a hurricane had passed through it. Cases were shattered, glass was all over the floor, and pools of water lay everywhere. Bookcases had collapsed, and some of the models were wrecked.

There was one model ship at the bottom of the stairs, broken into a thousand tiny pieces. Danny could guess which one it was.

Mrs. Gower was groaning and trying to sit up. Nicole and Danny ran to help her.

"Are you okay?" Danny asked the elderly lady.

She shook her head and looked all around them. "It's ruined!" she cried. "Look at this mess!" Then she held her head. "I don't know what happened," she said, firmly. "And I don't want to know. Just tell me one thing—is it ever likely to happen again?"

119

"No," Nicole promised her. "No, it won't happen again. It's finished."

"Thank goodness for that." Mrs. Gower stood up and looked down at them. "I don't want to sound rude, but I'd be very happy if I never saw you children in here again."

"Suits me," agreed Danny.

"Don't you want us to help you clean up?" Nicole offered. Danny groaned at this.

Mrs. Gower shook her head firmly. "I just want you to *go*. Please!"

"Suit yourself." Danny led the way out into the sunshine. He and Nicole were dripping wet. A woman with a load of shopping gave them a very funny look. Danny flashed her a quick smile. "Broken water main," he said cheerfully.

Their bicycles lay where they had dropped them. Nicole gave a sigh of relief. "I think we'd better go home and get changed," she said. "Before Mom sees us."

"You can say that again," Danny agreed.

"Then we can enjoy the rest of the day," Nicole said. "Play games."

"Right," Danny said, getting on his bike. "But I'll tell you one thing—no more tag for me!"

More exciting **FOUL PLAY** titles!

HANGMAN It looks as if there's a real hangman loose at Tiffany's slumber party.

HIDE-AND-SEEK (March 1993) With its twisting hallways and winding stairways, the old house seems perfect for a game of hide-and-seek. But in this game, the losers could disappear for good.

SIMON SAYS (May 1993) Everyone always does what Simon says—when it's Simon Brewster talking. What if Simon says kill?

When playing **_HANGMAN_** can really choke you . . .

When playing **_TAG_** has you running for your life . . .

When playing **_HIDE-AND-SEEK_** could get you lost forever . . .

When everyone always does what **_SIMON SAYS_** . . .

IT'S NOT JUST A GAME ANYMORE.

It's . . . **FOUL PLAY**